JOHN KESSEL

"Brilliantly intelligent, light-handed, and warm-hearted—a dazzler."
—Ursula K. Le Guin

"Kessel is . . . capable of the most artful and rigorous literary composition, but with a mischievous genius that inclines him toward speculative fiction. . . . He writes with subtlety and great wit . . . and his craftmanship is frequently absolutely brilliant. Plus, his sense of comedy is remarkable."
—*Publishers Weekly*

"Kessel's wit sparkles."
—*Entertainment Weekly*

"Kessel successfully walks the fine line between mordant farce and psychological realism. . . . Real people moving through an American reality that gets more and more surreal."
—Norman Spinrad, *Asimov's Science Fiction*

"Over the course of his career he's been a leader in American science fiction . . . at the same time he's stayed completely strange and idiosyncratic. His stories are singular experiences."
—Kim Stanley Robinson

"Quite possibly the best short story writer working in science fiction today."
—*Sci-Fi Weekly*

The Presidential Papers

Papers

plus

PM PRESS OUTSPOKEN AUTHORS SERIES

The Presidential Papers

plus

Imagining the Human Future: Up, Down, or Sideways

plus

The Last American

and much more

John Kessel

PM PRESS | 2024

"A Clean Escape" first appeared in *Isaac Asimov's Science Fiction* 9, no. 5 (May 1985): 170–81.

"The Franchise" first appeared in *Isaac Asimov's Science Fiction* 17, no. 9 (August 1993): 8–46.

"The President's Channel" first appeared in the Raleigh *News and Observer*, June 28, 1998.

"The Last American" first appeared in *Foundation: The International Review of Science Fiction* 100 (August 2007): 87–100.

"A Brief History of the War with Venus" is original to this volume.

"Imagining the Human Future: Up, Down, or Sideways," originally given as a speech, November 2001, appears here, slightly revised, for the first time.

ISBN (paperback): 979-8-88744-058-3
ISBN (ebook): 979-8-88744-067-5
LCCN: 2024930560

Series editor: Terry Bisson
Cover design by John Yates/www.stealworks.com
Author photo by Therese Anne Fowler
Insides by Jonathan Rowland

10 9 8 7 6 5 4 3 2 1

Printed in the USA

CONTENTS

A Clean Escape

"I've been thinking about devils. I mean
if there are devils in the world, if there are
people in the world who represent evil,
is it our duty to exterminate them?"
—John Cheever, "The Five-Forty-Eight"

As she sat in her office, waiting—for exactly what she did not
know—Dr. Evans hoped that it wasn't going to be another bad
day. She needed a cigarette and a drink. She swiveled the chair
around to face the closed venetian blinds beside her desk, leaned
back, and laced her hands behind her head. She closed her eyes
and breathed deeply. The air wafting down from the ventilator in
the ceiling smelled of machine oil. It was cold. Her face felt it, but
the bulky sweater kept the rest of her warm. Her hair felt greasy.
Several minutes passed. There was a knock at the door.

"Come in," she said absently.

Havelmann entered. He had the large body of an athlete gone
slightly soft, gray hair, and a lined face. At first glance he didn't
look sixty. His well-tailored blue suit badly needed pressing.

"Doctor?"

Evans stared at him for a moment. She would kill him. She
looked down at the desk, rubbed her forehead. "Sit down," she said.

She took the pack of cigarettes from her desk drawer. "Would you care to smoke?"

The old man accepted one. She watched him carefully. His brown eyes were rimmed with red; they looked apologetic.

"I smoke too much," he said. "But I can't quit."

She gave him a light. "More people around here are quitting every day."

Havelmann exhaled smoothly. "What can I do for you?"

What can I do for *you,* sir.

"First, I want to play a little game." Evans took a handkerchief out of her pocket. She moved a brass paperweight, a small model of the Lincoln Memorial, to the center of the desk blotter. "I want you to watch what I'm doing now."

Havelmann smiled. "Don't tell me—you're going to make it disappear, right?"

She tried to ignore him. She covered the paperweight with the handkerchief. "What's under this handkerchief?"

"Can we put a little bet on it?"

"Not this time."

"A paperweight."

"That's wonderful." Evans leaned back. "Now I want you to answer a few questions."

The old man looked around the office curiously: at the closed blinds, at the computer terminal and keyboard against the wall, at the pad of switches in the corner of the desk. His eyes came to rest on the mirror high in the wall opposite the window. "That's a two-way mirror."

Evans sighed. "No kidding."

"Are you recording this?"

"Does it matter to you?"

"I'd like to know. Common courtesy."

"Yes, we're being recorded. Now answer the questions."

Havelmann seemed to shrink in the face of her hostility. "Sure."

"How do you like it here?"

"It's okay. A little boring. A man couldn't even catch a disease here, from the looks of it, if you know what I mean. I don't mean any offense, Doctor. I haven't been here long enough to get the feel of the place."

Evans rocked slowly back and forth. "How do you know I'm a doctor?"

"Aren't you a doctor? I thought you were. This is a hospital, isn't it? So I figured when they sent me in to see you, you must be a doctor."

"I am a doctor. My name is Evans."

"Pleased to meet you, Dr. Evans."

She would kill him. "How long have you been here?"

The man tugged on his earlobe. "I must have just got here today. I don't think it was too long ago. A couple of hours. I've been talking to the nurses at their station."

What she wouldn't give for three fingers of Jack Daniels. She looked at him over the steeple of her fingers. "Such talkative nurses."

"I'm sure they're doing their jobs."

"I'm sure. Tell me what you were doing before you came to this . . . hospital."

"You mean right before?"

"Yes."

"I was working."

"Where do you work?"

"I've got my own company—ITG Computer Systems. We design programs for a lot of people. We're close to getting a big contract with Ma Bell. We swing that and I can retire by the time I'm forty—if Uncle Sam will take his hand out of my pocket long enough for me to count my change."

Evans made a note on her pad. "Do you have a family?"

Havelmann looked at her steadily. His gaze was that of an earnest young college student, incongruous on a man of his age. He stared at her as if he could not imagine why she would ask him these abrupt questions. She detested his weakness; it raised in her a fury that pushed her to the edge of insanity. It was already a bad day, and it would get worse.

"I don't understand what you're after," Havelmann said, with considerable dignity. "But just so your record shows the facts: I've got a wife, Helen, and two kids. Ronnie's nine and Susan's five. We have a nice big house and a Lincoln and a Porsche. I follow the Braves and I don't eat quiche. What else would you like to know?"

"Lots of things. Eventually I'll find them out." Evans tapped her pencil on the edge of the desk. "Is there anything you'd like to ask me? How you came to be here? How long you're going to have to stay? Who you are?"

Havelmann's voice went cold. "I know who I am."

"Who are you, then?"

"My name is Robert Havelmann."

"That's right," Dr. Evans said. "What year is it?"

Havelmann watched her warily, as if he were about to be tricked. "What are you talking about? It's 1984."

"What time of year?"

"Spring."

"How old are you?"

"Thirty-five."

"What do I have under this handkerchief?"

Havelmann looked at the handkerchief on the desk as if noticing it for the first time. His shoulders tightened and he looked suspiciously at her.

"How should I know?"

***

He was back again that afternoon, just as rumpled, just as innocent. How could a person get old and remain innocent? She could not remember things ever being that easy. "Sit down," she said.

"Thanks. What can I do for you, Doctor?"

"I want to follow up on the argument we had this morning."

Havelmann smiled. "Argument? This morning?"

"Don't you remember talking to me this morning?"

"I never saw you before."

Evans watched him coldly. Havelmann shifted in his chair.

"How do you know I'm a doctor?"

"Aren't you a doctor? They told me I should go in to see Dr. Evans in room 10."

"I see. If you weren't here this morning, where were you?"

Havelmann hesitated. "Let's see—I was at work. I remember telling Helen that I'd try to get home early. She's always complaining because I stay late. The company's pretty busy right now: big contract in the works. Susan's in the school play, and we have to be there by eight. And I want to get home in time to do some yard work. It looked like a good day for it."

Evans made a note. "What season is it?"

Havelmann fidgeted and looked at the window, where the blinds were still closed.

"Spring," he said. "Sunny, warm—very nice weather. The redbuds are just starting to come out."

Without a word Evans got out of her chair and opened the blinds, revealing a barren field swept with drifts of snow. Dead grass whipped in the strong wind, and clouds rolled in the sky.

Havelmann stared. His back straightened. He tugged at his earlobe.

"Isn't that a bitch. If you don't like the weather here—wait ten minutes."

"What about the redbuds?"

"This weather will probably kill them. I hope Helen made the kids wear their jackets."

Evans looked out the window. Nothing had changed. She drew the blinds and sat down again.

"What year is it?"

Havelmann adjusted himself in his chair, calm again. "What do you mean? It's 1984."

"Did you ever read that book?"

"Slow down a minute. What book?"

Evans wondered what he would do if she got up and ground her thumbs into his eyes. "The book by George Orwell titled *1984*." She forced herself to speak slowly. "Are you familiar with it?"

"Sure. We had to read it in college." Was there a trace of irritation beneath Havelmann's innocence? Evans sat as still as she could.

"I remember it made quite an impression on me," Havelmann continued.

"What kind of impression?"

"I expected something different from the professor. He was a bleeding-heart liberal. I expected some kind of bleeding-heart book. It wasn't like that at all."

"Did it make you uncomfortable?"

"It didn't tell me anything I didn't know already. It just showed what was wrong with collectivism. Communism represses the individual, destroys initiative. It claims it has the interests of the majority at heart. And it denies all human values. That's what I got out of *1984*, though to hear that professor talk about it, it was all about Nixon and Vietnam."

Evans kept still. Havelmann went on.

"I've seen the same mentality at work in business. The large corporations, they're just like the government. Big, slow. You could show them a way to save a billion, and they'd squash you like a bug because it's too much trouble to change."

"You sound like you've got some resentments," said Evans.

The old man smiled. "I do, don't I. I admit it. I've thought a lot about it. But I have faith in people. Someday I may just run for state assembly and see whether I can do some good."

Her pencil point snapped. She looked at Havelmann, who looked back at her. After a moment she focused her attention on the notebook. The broken point had left a black scar across her precise handwriting.

"That's a good idea," she said quietly, her eyes still lowered. "You still don't remember arguing with me this morning?"

"I never saw you before I walked in this door. What were we

supposed to be fighting about?"

He was insane. Evans almost laughed aloud at the thought—of course he was insane—why else would he be here? The question, she forced herself to consider rationally, was the nature of his insanity. She picked up the paperweight and handed it across to him. "We were arguing about this paperweight," she said. "I showed it to you, and you said you'd never seen it before."

Havelmann examined the paperweight. "Looks ordinary to me. I could easily forget something like this. What's the big deal?"

"You'll note that it's a model of the Lincoln Memorial."

"You probably got it at some gift shop. DC is full of junk like that."

"I haven't been to Washington in a long time."

"I wish I could avoid it. I live there. Bethesda, anyway."

Evans closed her notebook. "I have a possible diagnosis of your condition," she said.

"What condition?"

This time the laughter was harder to repress. Tears almost came to her eyes. She caught her breath and continued. "You exhibit the symptoms of Korsakoff syndrome. Have you ever heard of that?"

Havelmann looked as blank as a whitewashed wall. "No."

"Korsakoff syndrome is an unusual form of memory loss. Recorded cases go back to the late 1800s. There was a famous one in the 1970s—famous to doctors, I mean. A marine sergeant named Arthur Briggs. He was in his fifties, in good health aside from the lingering effects of alcoholism, and had been a career noncom until his discharge in the mid-sixties after twenty years in the service. He functioned normally until the early seventies, when he lost his memory of any events that occurred to him after

September 1944. He could remember in vivid detail, as if they had just happened, events up until that time. But of the rest of his life—nothing. Not only that, his continuing memory was affected so that he could remember events that occurred in the present only for a period of minutes, after which he would totally forget them."

"I can remember what happened to me right up until I walked into this room."

"That's what Sergeant Briggs told his doctors. To prove it he told them that World War II was going strong, that he was stationed in San Francisco in preparation for being sent to the Philippines, that it looked like the St. Louis Browns might finally win a pennant if they could hold on through September, and that he was twenty years old. He had the outlook and abilities of an intelligent twenty-year-old. He couldn't remember anything that happened to him longer than twenty minutes. The world had gone on, but he was permanently stuck in 1944."

"That's horrible."

"So it seemed to the doctor in charge—at first. Later he speculated that it might not be so bad. The man still had a current emotional life. He could still enjoy the present; it just didn't stick with him. He could remember his youth, and for him his youth had never ended. He never aged. He never saw his friends grow old and die; he never remembered that he himself had grown up to be a lonely alcoholic. His girlfriend was still waiting for him back in Columbia, Missouri. He was twenty years old forever. He had made a clean escape."

Evans opened a desk drawer and took out a hand mirror. "How old are you?" she asked.

Havelmann looked frightened. "Look, why are we doing—"

"How old are you?" Evans's voice was quiet but determined. Inside her a pang of joy threatened to break her heart.

"I'm thirty-five. What the hell—"

Shoving the mirror at him was as satisfying as firing a gun. Havelmann took it, glanced at her, then tentatively, like the most nervous of freshmen checking the grade on his final exam, looked at his reflection. "Jesus Christ," he said. He started to tremble.

"What happened? What did you do to me?" He got out of the chair, his expression contorted. "What did you do to me! I'm thirty-five! What happened?"

#

Dr. Evans stood in front of the mirror in her office. She was wearing her uniform. It was as rumpled as Havelmann's suit. She had the tunic unbuttoned and was feeling her left breast. She lay down on the floor and continued the examination. The lump was undeniable. No pain yet.

She sat up, reached for the pack of cigarettes on the desktop, fished out the last one, and lit it. She crumpled the pack and threw it at the wastebasket. Two points. She had been quite a basketball player in college, twenty years before. She lay back down and took a long drag on the cigarette, inhaling deeply, exhaling the smoke with force, with a sigh of exhaustion. She probably couldn't make it up and down the court a single time anymore.

She turned her head to look out the window. The blinds were open, revealing the same barren landscape that showed before. There was a knock at the door.

"Come in," she said.

Havelmann entered. He saw her lying on the floor, raised an eyebrow, grinned. "You're Dr. Evans?"

"I am."

"Can I sit here, or should I lie down too?"

"Do whatever you fucking well please."

He sat in the chair. He had not taken offense. "So what did you want to see me about?"

Evans got up, buttoned her tunic, sat in the swivel chair. She stared at him. "Have we ever met before?" she asked.

"No. I'm sure I'd remember."

He was sure he would remember. She would fucking kill him. He would remember that.

She ground out the last inch of cigarette. She felt her jaw muscles tighten; she looked down at the ashtray in regret. "Now I have to quit."

"I should quit. I smoke too much myself."

"I want you to listen to me closely now," she said slowly. "Don't respond until I'm finished. My name is Major D.S. Evans, and I am a military psychologist. This office is in the infirmary of NECDEC, the National Emergency Center for Defense Communications, located one thousand feet below a hillside in West Virginia. As far as we know we are the only surviving governmental body in the continental United States. The scene you see through this window is being relayed from a surface monitor in central Nebraska; by computer command I can connect us with any of the twelve monitors still functioning on the surface."

Evans turned to her keyboard and typed in a command; the scene through the window snapped to a shot of broken masonry and twisted steel reinforcement rods. The view was obscured by dust caked on the camera lens and by a heavy snowfall. Evans typed in an additional command and touched one of the switches on her desk. A blast of static, a hiss like frying bacon, came from the speaker.

"That's Dallas. The sound is a reading of the background radiation registered by detectors at the site of this camera." She typed in another command and the image on the "window" flashed through a succession of equally desolate scenes, holding ten seconds on each before switching to the next. A desert in twilight, motionless under low clouds; a murky underwater shot in which the remains of a building were just visible; a denuded forest half buried in snow; a deserted highway overpass. With each change of scene the loudspeaker stopped for a split second, then the hiss resumed.

Havelmann watched all of this soberly.

"This has been the state of the surface for a year now, ever since the last bombs fell. To our knowledge there are no human beings alive in North America—in the Northern Hemisphere, for that matter. Radio transmissions from South America, New Zealand, and Australia have one by one ceased in the last eight months. We have not observed a living creature above the level of an insect through any of our monitors since the beginning of the year. It is the summer of 2010. Although, considering the situation, counting years by the old system seems a little futile to me."

Dr. Evans slid open a desk drawer and took out a pistol. She placed it in the middle of the desk blotter and leaned back, her right hand touching the edge of the desk near the gun.

"You are now going to tell me that you never heard of any of this, and that you've never seen me before in your life," she said, "despite the fact that I have been speaking to you daily for two weeks and that you have had this explanation from me at least three times during that period. You are going to tell me that it is 1984 and that you are thirty-five years old, despite the absurdity of such a claim. You are going to feign amazement and confusion; the more I insist that you face these facts, the more you are going to become distressed. Eventually you will break down into tears and expect me to sympathize. You can go to hell."

Evans's voice had grown angrier as she spoke. She had to stop; it was almost more than she could do. When she resumed she was under control again. "If you persist in this sham, I may kill you. I assure you that no one will care if I do. You may speak now."

Havelmann stared at the window. His mouth opened and closed stupidly. How old he looked, how feeble. Evans felt a sudden surge of doubt. What if she were wrong? She had an image of herself as she might appear to him: arrogant, bitter, an incomprehensible inquisitor whose motives for tormenting him were a total mystery. She watched him. After a few minutes his mouth closed; the eyes blinked rapidly and were clear.

"Please. Tell me what you're talking about."

Evans shuddered. "The gun is loaded. Keep talking."

"What do you want me to say? I never heard of any of this. Only this morning I saw my wife and kids, and everything was all right. Now you give me this story about atomic war and 2010. What, have I been asleep for thirty years?"

"You didn't act very surprised to be here when you walked in. If you're so disoriented, how do you explain how you got here?"

The man sat heavily in the chair. "I don't remember. I guess I thought I came here—to the hospital, I thought—to get a check-up. I didn't think about it. You must know how I got here."

"I do. But I think you know, too, and you're just playing a game with me—with all of us. The others are worried, but I'm sick of it. I can see through you, so you may as well quit the act. You were famous for your sincerity, but I always suspected that was an act, too, and I'm not falling for it. You didn't start this game soon enough for me to be persuaded you're crazy, despite what the others may think."

Evans played with the butt of her dead cigarette. "Or this could be a delusional system," she continued. "You think you're in a hospital, and your disease has progressed to the point where you deny all facts that don't go along with your attempts to evade responsibility. I suppose in some sense such an insanity would absolve you. If that's the case, I should be more objective.

"Well, I can't. I'm failing my profession. Too bad." Emotion had drained away from her until, by the end, she felt as if she were speaking from across a continent instead of a desk.

"I still don't know what you're talking about. Where are my wife and kids?"

"They're dead."

Havelmann sat rigidly. The only sound was the hiss of the radiation detector. "Let me have a cigarette."

"There are no cigarettes left. I just smoked my last one." Evans touched the ashtray. "I made two cartons last a year."

Havelmann's gaze dropped. "How old my hands are! . . . Helen has lovely hands."

"Why are you going on with this charade?"

The old man's face reddened. "God damn you! Tell me what happened!"

"The famous Havelmann rage. Am I supposed to be frightened now?"

The hiss from the loudspeaker seemed to increase. Havelmann lunged for the gun. Evans snatched it and pushed back from the desk. The old man grabbed the paperweight and raised it to strike. She pointed the gun at him.

"Your wife didn't make the plane in time. She was at the western White House. I don't know where your damned kids were—probably vaporized with their own families. You, however, had Operation Kneecap to save you, Mr. President. Now sit down and tell me why you've been playing games, or I'll kill you right here and now. Sit down!"

A light seemed to dawn on Havelmann. "You're insane."

"Put the paperweight back on the desk."

He did. He sat.

"But you can't simply be crazy," Havelmann continued. "There's no reason why you should take me away from my home and subject me to this. This is some kind of plot. The government. The CIA."

"And you're thirty-five years old?"

Havelmann examined his hands again. "You've done something to me."

"And the camps? Administrative Order 31?"

"If I'm the president, then why are you quizzing me here? Why can't I remember a thing about it?"

"Stop it. Stop it right now," Evans said. She heard her voice for the first time. It sounded more like that of an old man than Havelmann's. "I can't take any more lies. I swear that I'll kill you. First it was the commander-in-chief routine, calisthenics, stiff upper lips and discipline. Then the big brother, let's have a whiskey and talk it over, son. Yessir, Mr. President."

Havelmann stared at her. He was going to make her kill him, and she knew she wouldn't be strong enough not to.

"Now you can't remember anything," she said. "Your boys are confused, they're fed up. Well, I'm fed up, too."

"If this is true, you've got to help me!"

"I don't give a rat's ass about helping you!" Evans shouted. "I'm interested in making you tell the truth! Don't you realize that we're dead? I don't care about your feeble sense of what's right and wrong; just tell me what's keeping you going. Who do you think you're going to impress? You think you've got an election to win? A place in history to protect? There isn't going to be any more history! History ended last August!

"So spare me the fantasy about the hospital and the nonexistent nurses' station. Someone with Korsakoff wouldn't make up that story. He would recognize the difference between a window and an HDTV screen. A dozen other slips. You're not a good enough actor."

Her hand trembled. The gun was heavy. Her voice trembled, too, and she despised herself for it. "Sometimes I think the only thing that's kept me alive is knowing I had half a pack of cigarettes left. That and the desire to make you crawl."

The old man sat looking at the gun in her hand. "I was the president?"

"No," said Evans. "I made it up."

His eyes seemed to sink farther back in the network of lines surrounding them.

"I started a war?"

Evans felt her heart race. "Stop lying! You sent the strike force; you ordered the preemptive launch."

"I'm old. How old am I?"

"You know how old—" She stopped. She could hardly catch her breath. She felt a sharp pain in her breast. "You're sixty-one."

"Jesus, Mary, Joseph."

"That's it? That's all you can say?"

Havelmann stared hollowly, then slowly, so slowly that at first it was not apparent what he was doing, lowered his head into his hands and began to cry. His sobs were almost inaudible over the hiss of the radiation detector. Evans watched him. She rested her elbows on the desk, steadying the gun with both hands. Havelmann's head shook in front of her. Despite his age, his gray hair was thick.

After a moment Evans reached over and switched off the loud-speaker. The hissing stopped.

Eventually Havelmann stopped crying. He raised his head. He looked dazed. His expression became unreadable. He looked at her and the gun. "Why are you pointing that gun at me?"

"Don't do this," said Evans. "Please."

"Do what? Who are you?"

Evans watched his face blur. Through her tears he looked like a much younger man. The gun drooped. She tried to lift it, but it was as if she were made of smoke—there was no substance to her, and it was all she could do to keep from dissipating, let alone kill anyone as clean and innocent as Robert Havelmann. He reached forward. He took the gun from her hand.

"Are you all right?" he asked.

#

Dr. Evans sat in her office, hoping that it wasn't going to be a bad day. The pain in her breast had not come that day, but she was out of cigarettes. She searched the desk on the odd chance she might have missed a pack, even a single butt, in the corner of one of the drawers. No luck.

She gave up and turned to face the window. The blinds were open, revealing the snow-covered field. She watched the clouds roll before the wind. It was dark. Winter. Nothing was alive.

"It's cold outside," she whispered.

There was a knock at the door. Dear god, leave me alone, she thought. Please leave me alone.

"Come in," she said.

The door opened and an old man in a rumpled suit entered. "Dr. Evans? I'm Robert Havelmann. What did you want to see me about?"

The Franchise

"Whoever wants to know the heart and mind
of America had better learn baseball."
—Jacques Barzun

1.

When George Herbert Walker Bush strode into the batter's box to face the pitcher they called the Franchise, it was the bottom of the second, and the Senators were already a run behind.

But Killebrew had managed a double down the right-field line and two outs later still stood on second in the bright October sunlight, waiting to be driven in. The bleachers were crammed full of restless fans in colorful shirts. Far behind Killebrew, Griffith Stadium's green center-field wall zigzagged to avoid the towering oak in Mrs. Mahan's backyard, lending the stadium its crazy dimensions. They said the only players ever to homer into that tree were Mantle and Ruth. George imagined how the stadium would erupt if he did it, drove the first pitch right out of the old ball yard, putting the Senators ahead in the first game of the 1959 World Series. If wishes were horses, his father had told him more than once, then beggars would ride.

George stepped into the box, ground in his back foot, squinted at the pitcher. The first pitch, a fastball, so surprised him that he didn't get his bat off his shoulder. Belt high, it split the middle of the plate, but the umpire called, "Ball!"

"Ball?" Schmidt, the Giants' catcher, grumbled.

"You got a problem?" the umpire said.

"Me? I got no problem." Schmidt tossed the ball back to the pitcher, who shook his head in histrionic Latin American dismay, as if bemoaning the sins of the world that he'd seen only too much of since he'd left Havana eleven years before. "But the Franchise, he no like."

George ignored them and set himself for the next pitch. The big Cuban went into his herky-jerky windup, deceptively slow, then kicked and threw. George was barely into his swing when the ball thwacked into the catcher's glove. "Steerike one!" the umpire called.

He was going to have to get around faster. The next pitch was another fastball, outside and high, but George had already triggered before the release and missed it by a foot, twisting himself around so that he almost fell over.

Schmidt took the ball out of his glove, showed it to George, and threw it back to the mound.

The next was a curve, outside by an inch. Ball two.

The next a fastball that somehow George managed to foul into the dirt.

The next a fastball up under his chin that had him diving into the dirt himself. Ball three. Full count.

An expectant murmur rose in the crowd, then fell to a profound silence, the silence of a church, of heaven, of a lover's secret heart. Was his father among them, breathless, hoping? Thousands awaited the next pitch. Millions more watched on television. Killebrew took a three-step lead off second. The Giants made no attempt to hold him on. The chatter from the Senators' dugout lit up. "Come on, George Herbert Walker Bush, bear down! Come on, Professor!"

George set himself, weight on his back foot. He cocked his bat, squinted out at the pitcher. The vainglorious Latino gave him a piratical grin, shook off Schmidt's sign. George felt his shoulders tense. Calm, boy, calm, he told himself. You've been shot at, you've faced Prescott Bush across a dining-room table—this is nothing but baseball. But instead of calm he felt panic, and as the Franchise went into his windup his mind stood blank as a stone.

The ball started out right for his head. George jerked back in a desperate effort to get out of the way as the pitch, a curve of prodigious sweep, dropped through the heart of the plate. "Steerike!" the umpire called.

Instantly the scene changed from hushed expectation to sudden movement. The crowd groaned. The players relaxed and began jogging off the field. Killebrew kicked the dirt and walked back to the dugout to get his glove. The organist started up. Behind the big Chesterfield sign in right, the scorekeeper slid another goose egg onto the board for the Senators. Though the whole thing was similar to moments he had experienced more times than he would care to admit during his ten years in the minors, the simple volume of thirty thousand voices sighing in disappointment because he, George Herbert Walker Bush, had failed, left him standing stunned at the plate with the bat limp in his clammy hands. They didn't get thirty thousand fans in Chattanooga.

Schmidt flipped the ball toward the mound. As the Franchise jogged past him, he flashed George that superior smile. "A magnificent swing," he said.

George stumbled back to the dugout. Lemon, heading out to left, shook his head. "Nice try, Professor," the shortstop Consolo said.

"Pull your jock up and get out to first," said Lavagetto, the manager. He spat a stream of tobacco juice onto the sod next to the end of the dugout. "Señor Fidel Castro welcomes you to the bigs."

2.

The Senators lost 7–1. Castro pitched nine innings, allowed four hits, struck out ten. George fanned three times. In the sixth, he let a low throw get by him; the runner ended up on third, and the Giants followed with four unearned runs.

In the locker room his teammates avoided him. Nobody had played well, but George knew they had him pegged as a choker. Lavagetto came through with a few words of encouragement. "We'll get 'em tomorrow," he said. George expected the manager to yank him for somebody who at least wouldn't cost them runs on defense. When he left without saying anything, George was grateful to him for at least letting him go another night before getting benched.

Barbara and the boys had been in the stands, but had gone home. They would be waiting for him. He didn't want to go. The stadium was empty by the time he walked out through the tunnels to the street. His head was filled with images from the game. Castro had toyed with him; he no doubt enjoyed humiliating the son of a US senator. The Cuban's look of heavy-lidded disdain sparked an unaccustomed rage in George. It wasn't good sportsmanship. You played hard, and you won or lost, but you didn't rub the other guy's nose in it. That was bush league, and George, despite his unfortunate name, was anything but bush.

That George should end up playing first base for the Washington Senators in the 1959 World Series was the result of as improbable a sequence of events as had ever conspired to make a man of a rich boy. The key moment had come on a June Saturday in 1948, when he had shaken the hand of Babe Ruth.

That June morning the Yale baseball team was to play Brown, but before the game a ceremony was held to honor Ruth, donating the manuscript of his autobiography to the university library. George, captain of the Yale squad, would accept the manuscript. As he stood at the microphone set up between the pitcher's mound and second base, he was stunned by the gulf between the pale hulk standing before him and the legend he represented. Ruth, only fifty-three on that spring morning, could hardly speak for the throat cancer that was killing him. He gasped out a few words, stooped over, rail thin, no longer the giant he had been in the twenties. George took his hand. It was dry and papery and brown as a leaf in fall. Through his grip George felt the contact with glorious history, with feats of heroism that would never be matched, with 714 home runs and 1,356 extra-base hits, with a lifetime slugging percentage of .690, with the called shot and the sixty-homer season and the 1927 Yankees and the curse of the Red Sox. An electricity surged up his arm and directly into his soul. Ruth had accomplished as much, in his way, as a man could accomplish in a life; more, even, George realized to his astonishment, than had his father, Prescott Bush. He stood there stunned, charged with an unexpected, unasked-for purpose.

He had seen death in the war, had tasted it in the blood that streamed from his forehead when he'd struck it against the tail of the TBM Avenger as he parachuted out of the flaming bomber over the Pacific in 1943. He had felt death's hot breath on his back as he frantically paddled the yellow rubber raft away from Chichi Jima against waves pushing him back into the arms of the Japanese, had felt death draw away and offered up a silent prayer when the conning tower of the USS *Finback* broke through the agitated seas to save him from a savage fate—to, he always knew, some higher purpose. He had imagined that purpose to be business or public service. Now he recognized that he had been seeing his future through his father's eyes, that in fact his fate lay elsewhere. It lay between the chalk lines of a playing field, on the greensward of the infield, among the smells of pine tar and saw-dust and chewing tobacco and liniment. He could feel it through the tendons of the fleshless hand of Babe Ruth that he held in his own at that very instant.

The day after he graduated from Yale he signed, for no bonus, with the Cleveland Indians.

Ten years later, George had little to show for his bold choice. He wasn't the best first baseman you ever saw. Nobody stopped him on the street to ask for his autograph. He never made the Indians, and got traded to the Browns. He hung on, bouncing up and down the farm systems of seventh- and eighth-place teams. Every spring he went to Florida with high expectations, every April he started the season in Richmond, in Rochester, in Chattanooga. Just two months earlier he had considered packing it in and looking for another career. Then a series of miracles happened.

Chattanooga was the farm team for the Senators, who hadn't won a pennant since 1933. For fifteen years, under their notori-ously cheap owner Clark Griffith, they'd been as bad as you could get. But in 1959 their young third baseman, Harmon Killebrew, hit forty-two home runs. Sluggers Jim Lemon and Roy Sievers had career years. A big Kansas boy named Bob Allison won rookie of the year in center field. Camilo Pascual won twenty-two games, struck out 215 men. A kid named Jim Kaat won seventeen. Everything broke right, including Mickey Mantle's leg. After hovering a couple of games over .500 through the All-Star break, the Senators got hot in August, won ninety games, and finished one ahead of the Yankees.

When, late in August, right fielder Albie Pearson got hurt, Lavagetto switched Sievers to right, and there was George Bush, thirty-five years old, starting at first base for the American League champions in the World Series against the New York Giants.

The Giants were heavy favorites. Who would bet against a team that fielded Willie Mays, Orlando Cepeda, Willie McCovey, Felipe Alou, and pitchers like Johnny Antonelli, the fireballer Toothpick Sam Jones, and the Franchise, Fidel Castro? If, prior to the series, you'd told George the Senators were doomed, he would not have disagreed with you. After game one he had no reason to think otherwise.

He stood outside the stadium looking for a cab, contemplating his series record—one game, 0 for 4, one error—when a pale old man in a loud sports coat spoke to him. "Just be glad you're here," the man said.

The man had watery blue eyes, a sharp face. He was thin enough to look ill. "I beg your pardon?"

"You're the fellow the Nats called up in September, right? Remember, even if you never play another inning, at least you were there. You felt the sun on your back, got dirt on your hands, saw the stands full of people from down on the field. Not many get even that much."

"The Franchise made me look pretty sick."

"You have to face him down."

"Easier said than done."

"Don't say—do."

"Who are you, old man?"

The man hesitated. "Name's Weaver. I'm a—a fan. Yes, I'm a baseball fan." He touched the brim of his hat and walked away.

George thought about it on the cab ride home. It did not make him feel much better. When he got back to the cheap furnished apartment they were renting, Barbara tried to console him.

"My father wasn't there, was he?" George said.

"No. But he called after the game. He wants to see you."

"Probably wants to give me a few tips on how to comport myself. Or maybe just gloat."

Bar came around behind his chair, rubbed his tired shoulders. George got up and switched on the television. While he waited for it to warm up, the silence stretched. He faced Barbara. She had put on a few pounds over the years, but he remembered the first time he'd seen her across the dance floor in the red dress. He was seventeen. "What do you think he wants?"

"I don't know, George."

"I haven't seen him around in the last ten years. Have you?"

The TV had warmed up, and Prescott Bush's voice blared out from behind George. "I hope the baseball Senators win," he was saying. "They've had a better year than the Democratic ones."

George twisted down the volume, stared for a moment at his father's handsome face, then snapped it off. "Give me a drink," he told Barbara. He noticed the boys standing in the doorway, afraid. Barbara hesitated, poured a scotch and water.

"And don't stint on the scotch!" George yelled. He turned to George Jr.. "What are you looking at, you little weasel! Go to bed."

Barbara slammed down the glass so hard the scotch splashed the counter. "What's got into you, George? You're acting like a crazy man."

George took the half-empty glass from her hand. "My father's got into me, that's what. He got into me thirty years ago, and I can't get him out."

Barbara shot him a look in which disgust outweighed pity and went back to the boys' room. George slumped in the armchair, picked up a copy of *Look*, and leafed through the pages. He stopped on a Gillette razor ad. Castro smiled out from the page, dark hair slicked back, chin sleek as a curveball, a devastating blonde leaning on his shoulder. Look Sharp, Feel Sharp, *Be* Sharp, the ad told George.

Castro. What did he know about struggle? Yet that egomaniac lout was considered a hero, while he, George Herbert Walker Bush, who at twenty-four had been at the head of every list of the young men most likely to succeed, had accomplished precisely nothing.

People who didn't know any better had assumed that because of his background, money, and education he would grow to be one of the ones who told others what it was necessary for them to do, but George had come to realize, with a surge of panic, that he was not special. His moment of communion with Babe Ruth had been a delusion. Ruth was another type of man. Perhaps Ruth was used by the teams that bought and sold him, but inside Ruth was some compulsion that drove him to be larger than the uses to which he was put, so that in the end he remade those uses, remade the game itself.

George, talented though he had seemed, had no such size. The vital force that had animated his grandfather George Herbert Walker, after whom he was named, the longing after mystery that had impelled the metaphysical poet George Herbert, after whom that grandfather had been named, had diminished into a trickle in George Herbert Walker Bush. No volcanic forces surged inside him. When he listened late in the night, all he could hear of his soul was a thin keening, the sound of a bug trapped in a jar. *Let me go*, it whispered. *Let me go*.

That old man at the ballpark was wrong. It was not enough, not nearly enough, just to be there. What good was it to stand on first base in the World Series if you came away from it a laughing-stock? To have your father call you not because you were a hero, but only to remind you once again what a failure you are.

"I'll be damned if I go see him," George muttered to the empty room.

3.

President Nixon called Lavagetto in the middle of the night with a suggestion for the batting order in the second game. "Put Bush in the number-five slot," Nixon said.

Lavagetto wondered how he was supposed to tell the President of the United States that he was out of his mind. "Yessir, Mr. President."

"See, that way you get another right-handed batter at the top of the order."

Lavagetto considered pointing out to the president that the Giants were pitching a right-hander in game two. "Yessir, Mr. President," Lavagetto said. His wife was awake now, looking at him with irritation from her side of the bed. He put his hand over the mouthpiece and said, "Go to sleep."

"Who is it at this hour?"

"The president of the United States."

"Uh-huh."

Nixon had some observations about one-run strategies. Lavagetto agreed with him until he could get him off the line. He looked at his alarm clock. It was half past two.

Nixon had sounded full of manic energy. His voice dripped assurance. He wondered if Nixon was a drinking man. Walter Winchell said that Eisenhower's death had shoved the veep into an office he was unprepared to hold.

Lavagetto shut off the light and lay back down, but he couldn't sleep. What about Bush? Damn Pearson for getting himself hurt. Bush should be down in the minors where he belonged. He looked to be cracking under the pressure like a ripe melon.

But maybe the guy could come through, prove himself. He was no kid. Lavagetto knew from personal experience how, in the Series, the unexpected could turn on the swing of the bat. He recalled that fourth game of the '47 series, his double to right field that cost Floyd Bevens his no-hitter, and the game. Lavagetto had been a thirty-four-year-old utility infielder for the luckless Dodgers, an aging substitute playing out the string at the end of his career. In that whole season he'd hit only one other double. When he'd seen that ball twist past the right fielder, the joy had shot through his chest like lightning. The Dodger fans had gone crazy; his teammates had leapt all over him laughing and shouting and swearing like Durocher himself.

He remembered that, despite the miracle, the Dodgers had lost the Series to the Yankees in seven.

Lavagetto turned over. First in War, First in Peace, Last in the American League . . . that was the Washington Senators. He hoped young Jim Kaat was getting more sleep than he was.

4.

Tuesday afternoon, in front of a wild capacity crowd, young Jim Kaat pitched one of the best games by a rookie in the history of the Series. The twenty-year-old left-hander battled Toothpick Sam Jones pitch for pitch, inning for inning. Jones struggled with his control, walking six in the first seven innings, throwing two wild pitches. If it weren't for the over-eagerness of the Senators, swinging at balls a foot out of the strike zone, they would surely have scored; instead they squandered opportunity after opportunity. The fans grew restless. They could see it happening, in sour expectation of disaster built up over twenty-five frustrated years: Kaat would pitch brilliantly, and it would be wasted because the Giants would score on some bloop single.

Through seven the game stayed a scoreless tie. By some fluke George could not fathom, Lavagetto, instead of benching him, had moved him up in the batting order. Though he was still without a hit, he had been playing superior defense. In the seventh he snuffed a Giant uprising when he dove to snag a line drive off the bat of Schmidt for the third out, leaving runners at second and third.

Then, with two down in the top of the eighth, Cepeda singled. George moved in to hold him on. Kaat threw over a couple of times to keep the runner honest, with Cepeda trying to judge Kaat's move. Mays took a strike, then a ball. Cepeda edged a couple of strides away from first.

Kaat went into his stretch, paused, and whipped the ball to first, catching Cepeda leaning the wrong way. Picked off! But Cepeda, instead of diving back, took off for second. George whirled and threw hurriedly. The ball sailed over Consolo's head into left field, and Cepeda went to third. E-3.

Kaat was shaken. Mays hit a screamer between first and second. George dove, but it was by him, and Cepeda jogged home with the lead.

Kaat struck out McCovey, but the damage was done. "You bush-league clown!" a fan yelled. George's face burned. As he trotted off the field, from the Giants' dugout came Castro's shout: "A heroic play, Mr. Rabbit!"

George wanted to keep going through the dugout and into the clubhouse. On the bench his teammates were conspicuously silent. Consolo sat down next to him. "Shake it off," he said. "You're up this inning."

George grabbed his bat and moved to the end of the dugout. First up in the bottom of the eighth was Sievers. He got behind 0–2, battled back as Jones wasted a couple, then fouled off four straight strikes until he'd worked Jones for a walk. The organist played charge lines and the crowd started chanting. Lemon moved Sievers to second. Killebrew hit a drive that brought the people to their feet screaming before it curved just outside the left-field foul pole, then popped out to short. He threw down his bat and stalked back toward the dugout.

"C'mon, Professor," Killebrew said as he passed Bush in the on-deck circle. "Give yourself a reason for being here."

Jones was a scary right-hander with one pitch: the heater. In his first three at-bats George had been overpowered; by the last he'd managed a walk. This time he went up with a plan: he was going to take the first pitch, get ahead in the count, then drive the ball.

The first pitch was a fastball just high.

Make contact. Don't force it. Go with the pitch.

The next was another fastball; George swung as soon as Jones let it go and sent a line drive over the third baseman's head. The crowd roared, and he was halfway down the first-base line when the third-base umpire threw up his hands and yelled, "Foul ball!"

He caught his breath, picked up his bat, and returned to the box. Sievers jogged back to second. Schmidt, standing with his hands on his hips, didn't look at George. From the Giants' dugout George heard, "Kiss your luck goodbye, you effeminate rabbit! You rich man's table leavings! You are devoid of even the makings of guts!"

George stepped out of the box. Castro had come down the dugout to the near end and was leaning out, arms braced on the field, hurling his abuse purple-faced. Rigney and the pitching coach had him by the shoulders, tugging him back. George turned away, feeling a cold fury in his belly.

He would show them all. He forgot to calculate, swept by rage. He set himself as far back in the box as possible. Jones took off his cap, wiped his forearm across his brow, and leaned over to check the signs. He shook off the first, then nodded and went into his windup.

As soon as he released George swung, and was caught completely off balance by a changeup. "Strike two, you shadow of a man!" Castro shouted. "Unnatural offspring of a snail and a worm! Strike two!"

Jones tempted him with an outside pitch; George didn't bite. The next was another high fastball; George started, then checked his swing. "Ball!" the home-plate ump called. Fidel booed. Schmidt argued, the ump shook his head. Full count.

George knew he should look for a particular pitch, in a particular part of the plate. After ten years of professional ball, this ought to be second nature, but Jones was so wild he didn't have a clue. George stepped out of the box, rubbed his hands on his pants. "Yes, wipe your sweaty hands, mama's boy! You have all the machismo of a bankbook!"

The rage came to his defense. He picked a decision out of the air, arbitrary as the breeze: fastball, outside.

Jones went into his windup. He threw his body forward, whipped his arm high over his shoulder. Fastball, outside. George swiveled his hips through the box, kept his head down, extended his arms. The contact of the bat with the ball was so slight he wasn't sure he'd hit it at all. A line drive down the right-field line, hooking as it rose, hooking, hooking . . . curling just inside the foul pole into the stands 320 feet away.

The fans exploded. George, feeling rubbery, jogged around first, toward second. Sievers pumped his fist as he rounded third; the Senators were up on their feet in the dugout shouting and slapping each other. Jones had his hands on his hips, head down and back to the plate. George rounded third and jogged across home, where he was met by Sievers, who slugged him in the shoulder, and the rest of his teammates in the dugout, who laughed and slapped his butt.

The crowd began to chant, "SEN-a-TOR, SEN-a-TOR." After a moment George realized they were chanting for him. He climbed out of the dugout again and tipped his hat, scanning the stands for Barbara and the boys. As he did he saw his father in the presidential box, leaning over to speak into the ear of the cheering President Nixon. He felt a rush of hope, ducked his head, and got back into the dugout.

Kaat held the Giants in the ninth, and the Senators won, 2–1.

In the locker room after the game, George's teammates whooped and slapped him on the back. Chuck Stobbs, the clubhouse comic, called him "the Bambino." For a while George hoped that his father might come down to congratulate him. Instead, for the first time in his career, reporters swarmed around him. They fired flashbulbs in salvoes. They pushed back their hats, flipped open their notebooks, and asked him questions.

"What's it feel like to win a big game like this?"

"I'm just glad to be here. I'm not one of these winning-is-everything guys."

"They're calling you the Senator. Your father is a senator. How do you feel about that?"

"I guess we're both senators," George said. "He just got to Washington a little sooner than I did."

They liked that a lot. George felt the smile on his face like a frozen mask. For the first time in his life he was aware of the muscles it took to smile, as tense as if they were lifting a weight.

After the reporters left he showered. George wondered what his father had been whispering into the president's ear, while everyone around him cheered. Some sarcastic comment? Some irrelevant political advice?

When he got back to his locker, toweling himself dry, he found a note lying on the bench. He opened it eagerly. It read:

To the Effeminate Rabbit:
Even the rodent has his day. But not when the eagle pitches.

Sincerely,
Fidel Alejandro Castro Ruz

5.

That Fidel Castro would go so far out of his way to insult George Herbert Walker Bush would come as no surprise to anyone who knew him. Early in Castro's first season in the majors, a veteran Phillies reliever, after watching Fidel warm up, approached the young Cuban. "Where did you get that curve?" he asked incredulously.

"From you," said Fidel. "That's why you don't have one."

But sparking his reaction to Bush was more than simple egotism. Fidel's antipathy grew from circumstances of background and character that made such animosity as inevitable as the rising of the sun in the east of Oriente province where he had been born thirty-two years before.

Like George Herbert Walker Bush, Fidel was the son of privilege, but a peculiarly Cuban form of privilege, as different from the blue-blooded Bush variety as the hot and breathless climate of Oriente was from chilly New England. Like Bush, Fidel endured a father as parsimonious with his warmth as those New England winters. Young Fidelito grew up well-acquainted with the back of Angel Castro's hand, the jeers of classmates who tormented him and his brother Raúl for their illegitimacy. Though Angel Castro owned two thousand acres and had risen from common sugarcane laborer to local caudillo, he did not possess the easy assurance of the rich of Havana, for whom Oriente was the Cuban equivalent of Alabama. The Castros were peasants. Fidel's father was illiterate, his mother a maid. No amount of money could erase Fidel's bastardy.

This history raged in Fidelito. Always in a fight, alternating boasts with moody silences, he longed for accomplishment in a fiery way that cast the longing of Bush to impress his own father into a sickly shadow. At boarding school in Santiago, he sought the praise of his teachers and admiration of his schoolmates. At Belen, Havana's exclusive Jesuit preparatory school, he became the champion athlete of all of Cuba. "El Loco Fidel," his classmates called him as, late into the night, at an outdoor court under a light swarming with insects, he would practice basketball shots until his feet were torn bloody and his head swam with forlorn images of the ball glancing off the iron rim.

At the University of Havana, between the scorching expanses of the baseball and basketball seasons, Fidel toiled over the scorching expanse of the law books. He sought triumph in student politics as he did in sports. In the evenings he met in tiny rooms with his comrades and talked about junk pitches and electoral strategy, about the reforms that were only a matter of time because the people's will could not be forever thwarted. They were on the side of history. Larger than even the largest of men, history would overpower anyone unless, like Fidel, he aligned himself with it so as not to be swept under by the tidal force of its inescapable currents.

In the spring of 1948, at the same time George Herbert Walker Bush was shaking the hand of Babe Ruth, these currents transformed Fidel's life. He was being scouted by several major-league teams. In the university he had gained control of his fastball and given birth to a curve of so monstrous an arc that Alex Pompez, the Giants' scout, reported that the well-spoken law student owned "a hook like Bo Peep." More significantly, Pirates scout Howie Haak observed that Fidel "could throw and think at the same time."

Indeed Fidel could think, though no one could come close to guessing the content of his furious thought. A war between glory and doom raged within him. Fidel's fury to accomplish things threatened to keep him from accomplishing anything at all. He had made enemies. In the late forties, student groups punctuated elections for head of the law-school class with assassinations. Rival political gangs fought in the streets. Events drove Fidel toward a crisis. And so, on a single day in 1948, he abandoned his political aspirations, quit school, married his lover, the fair Mirta Díaz-Balart, and signed a contract with the New York Giants.

It seemed a fortunate choice. In his rookie year he won fifteen games. After he took the Cy Young Award and was named MVP of the 1951 Series, the sportswriters dubbed him "the Franchise." This past season he had won twenty-nine. He earned, and squandered, a fortune. Controversy dogged him, politics would not let him go, the uniform of a baseball player at times felt much too small. His brother Raúl was imprisoned when Batista overthrew the government to avoid defeat in the election of 1952. Fidel made friends among the expatriates in Miami. He protested US policies. His alternative nickname became "the Mouth."

But all along Fidel knew his politics was mere pose. His spouting off to sports reporters did nothing compared to what money might do to help the guerrillas in the Sierra Maestra. Yet he had no money.

After the second game of the Series, instead of returning to the hotel, Fidel took a cab down to the Mall. He needed to be alone. It was early evening when he got out at the Washington Monument. The sky beyond the Lincoln Memorial shone orange and purple. The air still held some of the sultry heat of summer, like an evening in Havana. But this was a different sort of capital. These North Americans liked to think of themselves as clean, rational men of law instead of passion, a land of Washingtons and Lincolns, but away from the public buildings DC was still a southern city full of ex-slaves. Fidel looked down the Mall toward the bright Capitol, white and towering as a wedding cake, and wondered what he might have become had he continued law school. At one time he had imagined himself the George Washington of his own country, a liberating warrior. The true heir of José Martí, scholar, poet, and revolutionary. Like Martí he admired the idealism of the United States, but like him he saw its dark side. Here at the Mall, however, you could almost forget about that in an atmosphere of bogus Greek democracy, of liberty and justice for all. You might even forget that liberty could be bought and sold, a franchise purchasable for cold cash.

Fidel walked along the pool toward the Lincoln Memorial. The floodlights lit up the white columns, and inside shone upon the brooding figure of Lincoln. Despite his cynicism, Fidel was caught by the sight of it. He had been to Washington only once before, for the All-Star Game in 1956. He remembered walking through Georgetown with Mirta on his arm, feeling tall and handsome, ignoring the scowl of the maître d' in the restaurant who clearly disapproved of two such dark ones in his establishment.

He'd triumphed but was not satisfied. He had forced others to admit his primacy through the power of his will. He had shown them, with his strong arm, the difference between right and wrong. He was the Franchise. He climbed up the steps into the Memorial, read the words of Lincoln's Second Inaugural address engraved on the wall. THE PROGRESS OF OUR ARMS UPON WHICH ALL ELSE CHIEFLY DEPENDS IS AS WELL KNOWN TO THE PUBLIC AS TO MYSELF . . . But he was still the crazy Cuban, taken little more seriously than Desi Arnaz, and the minute that arm that made him a useful commodity should begin to show signs of weakening—in that same minute he would be undone. IT MAY SEEM STRANGE THAT ANY MEN SHOULD DARE TO ASK A JUST GOD'S ASSISTANCE IN WRINGING THEIR BREAD FROM THE SWEAT OF OTHER MEN'S FACES BUT LET US JUDGE NOT THAT WE BE NOT JUDGED.

Judge not? Perhaps Lincoln could manage it, but Fidel was a different sort of man.

In the secrecy of his mind Fidel could picture another world than the one he lived in. The marriage of love to Mirta had long since gone sour, torn apart by Fidel's lust for renown on the ball field and his lust for the astonishing women who fell like fruit from the trees into the laps of players such as he. More than once he felt grief over his faithlessness. He knew his solitude to be just punishment. That was the price of greatness, for, after all, greatness was a crime and deserved punishment.

Mirta was gone now, and their son with her. She worked for the hated Batista. He thought of Raúl languishing in Batista's prison on the Isle of Pines. Batista, embraced by this United States that ran Latin America like a company store. Raúl suffered for the people, while Fidel ate in four-star restaurants and slept with a different woman in every city, throwing away his youth, and the money he earned, on excrement.

He looked up into the great sad face of Lincoln. He turned from the monument to stare out across the Mall toward the gleaming white shaft of the Washington obelisk. It was full night now. Time to amend his life.

6.

The headline in the *Post* the next morning read, SENATOR BUSH EVENS SERIES. The story mentioned that Prescott Bush had shown up in the sixth inning and sat beside Nixon in the presidential box. But nothing more.

Bar decided not to go up to New York for the middle games of the Series. George traveled with the team to the Roosevelt Hotel. The home run had done something for him. He felt a new confidence.

The game-three starters were the veteran southpaw Johnny Antonelli for the Giants and Pedro Ramos for the Senators. The echoes of the national anthem had hardly faded when Allison led off for the Senators with a home run into the short porch in left field. The Polo Grounds fell dead silent. The Senators scored three runs in the first; George did his part, hitting a changeup into right center for a double, scoring the third run of the inning.

In the bottom half of the first the Giants came right back, tying it up on Mays's three-run homer.

After that the Giants gradually wore Ramos down, scoring a single run in the third and two in the fifth. Lavagetto pulled him for a pinch hitter in the sixth with George on third and Consolo at first, two outs. But Aspromonte struck out, ending the inning. Though Castro heckled George mercilessly throughout the game and the brash New York fans joined in, he played above himself. The Giants eventually won, 8–3, but George went three for five. Despite his miserable first game he was batting .307 for the Series. Down two games to one, the Washington players felt the loss, but had stopped calling him "George Herbert Walker Bush" and started calling him "the Senator."

7.

Lavagetto had set an eleven o'clock curfew, but Billy Consolo persuaded George to go out on the town. The Hot Corner was a dive on Seventh Avenue with decent Italian food and cheap drinks. George ordered a club soda and tried to get into the mood. Ramos moaned about the plate umpire's strike zone, and Consolo changed the subject.

Consolo had been a bonus boy; in 1953 the Red Sox had signed him right out of high school for $50,000. He had never panned out. George wondered if Consolo's career had been any easier to take than his own. At least nobody had hung enough expectations on George for him to be called a flop.

Stobbs was telling a story. "So the Baseball Annie says to him, 'But will you respect me in the morning?' and the shortstop says, 'Oh, baby, I'll respect you like crazy!'"

While the others were laughing, George headed for the men's room. Passing the bar, he saw, in a corner booth, Fidel Castro talking to a couple of men in slick suits. Castro's eyes flicked over him but registered no recognition.

When George came out the men in suits were in heated conversation with Castro. In the back of the room somebody dropped a quarter into the jukebox, and Elvis Presley's slinky "Money Honey" blared out. Bush had no use for rock and roll. He sat at the table, ignored his teammates' conversation, and kept an eye on Castro. The Cuban was strenuously making some point, stabbing the tabletop with his index finger. After a minute George noticed that someone at the bar was watching them, too. It was the pale old man he had seen at Griffith Stadium.

On impulse, George went up to him. "Hello, old-timer. You really must be a fan, if you followed the Series up here. Can I buy you a drink?"

The man turned decisively from watching Castro, as if deliberately putting aside some thought. He seemed about to smile but did not. Small red splotches colored his face. "Buy me a ginger ale."

George ordered a ginger ale and another club soda and sat on the next stool. "Money, honey, if you want to get along with me," Elvis sang.

The old man sipped his drink. "You had yourself a couple of good games," he said. "You're in the groove."

"I just got some lucky breaks."

"Don't kid me. I know how it feels when it's going right. You know just where the next pitch is going to be, and there it is. Somebody hits a line drive right at you, you throw out your glove and snag it without even thinking. You're in the groove."

"It comes from playing the game a long time."

The old man snorted. "Do you really believe that guff? Or are you just trying to hide something?"

"What do you mean? I've spent ten years playing baseball."

"And you expect me to believe you still don't know anything about it? Experience doesn't explain the groove." The man looked as if he were watching something far away. "When you're in that groove you're not playing the game, the game is playing you."

"But you have to plan your moves."

The old man looked at him as if he were from Mars. "Do you plan your moves when you're making love to your wife?" He finished his ginger ale, took another look back at Castro, then left.

Everyone, it seemed, knew what was wrong with him. George felt steamed. As if that wasn't enough, as soon as he returned to the table Castro's pals left and the Cuban swaggered over to George, leaned into him, and blew cigar smoke into his face. "I know you, George Herbert Walker Bush," he said, "Sen-a-tor Rabbit. The rich man's son."

George pushed him away. "You know, I'm beginning to find your behavior darned unconscionable, compadre."

"I stand here quaking with fear," Castro said. He poked George in the chest. "Back home in Birán we had a pen for the pigs. The gate of this pen was in disrepair. But it is still a fact, Senator Rabbit, that the splintered wooden gate of that pigpen, squealing on its rusted hinges, swung better than you."

Consolo started to get up, but George put a hand on his arm. "Say, Billy, our Cuban friend here didn't by any chance help you pick out this restaurant tonight, did he?"

"What, are you crazy? Of course not."

"Too bad. I thought if he did, we could get some good Communist food here."

The guys laughed. Castro leaned over.

"Very funny, Machismo Zero." His breath reeked of cigar smoke, rum, and garlic. "I guarantee that after tomorrow's game you will be even funnier."

8.

Fidel had never felt sharper than he did during his warm-ups the afternoon of the fourth game. It was a cool fall day, partial overcast with a threat of rain, a breeze blowing out to right. The chilly air only invigorated him. Never had his curve had more bite, his screwball more movement. His arm felt supple, his legs strong. As he strode in from the bullpen to the dugout, squinting out at the apartment buildings on Coogan's Bluff towering over the stands, a great cheer rose from the crowd.

Before the echoes of the national anthem had died he walked the first two batters, on eight pitches. The fans murmured. Schmidt came out to talk with him. "What's wrong?"

"Nothing is wrong," Fidel said, sending him back.

He retired Lemon on a pop fly and Killebrew on a fielder's choice. Bush came to the plate with two outs and men on first and second. The few Washington fans who had braved the Polo Grounds set up a chant: "SEN-a-TOR, SEN-a-TOR!"

Fidel studied Bush. Beneath Bush's bravado he could see panic in every motion of the body he wore like an ill-fitting suit. Fidel struck him out on three pitches.

Kralick held the Giants scoreless through three innings.

As the game progressed, Fidel's own personal game, the game of pitcher and batter, settled into a pattern. Fidel mowed down the batters after Bush in the order with predictable dispatch, but fell into trouble each time he faced the top of the order, getting just enough outs to bring Bush up with men on base and the game in the balance. He did this four times in the first seven innings.

Each time Bush struck out.

In the middle of the seventh, after Bush fanned to end the inning, Mays sat down next to Fidel on the bench. "What the hell do you think you're doing?"

Mays was the only player on the Giants whose stature rivaled that of the Franchise. Fidel, whose success came as much from craft as physical prowess, could not but admit that Mays was the most beautiful ballplayer he had ever seen. "I'm shutting out the Washington Senators in the fourth game of the World Series," Fidel said.

"What's this mickey mouse with Bush? You trying to make him look bad?"

"One does not have to try very hard."

"Well, cut it out—before you make a mistake with Killebrew or Sievers."

Fidel looked him dead in the eyes. "I do not make mistakes."

The Giants entered the ninth with a 3–0 lead. Fidel got two quick outs, then gave up a single to Sievers and walked Lemon and Killebrew to load the bases. Bush, at bat, represented the lead run. Schmidt called time and came out again. Rigney hurried out from the dugout, and Mays, to the astonishment of the crowd, came all the way in from center. "Yank him," he told Rigney.

Rigney looked exasperated. "Who's managing this team, Willie?"

"He's setting Bush up to be the goat."

Rigney looked at Fidel. Fidel looked at him. "Just strike him out," the manager said.

Fidel rubbed up the ball and threw three fastballs through the heart of the plate. Bush missed them all. By the last strike the New York fans were screaming, rocking the Polo Grounds with a parody of the Washington chant: "Sen-a-TOR, Sen-a-TOR, BUSH BUSH, BUSH!" and exploding into fits of laughter. The Giants led the series, 3–1.

9.

George made the cabbie drop him off at the corner of Broadway and Pine, in front of the old Trinity Church. He walked down Wall Street through crowds of men in dark suits, past the Stock Exchange to the offices of Brown Brothers, Harriman. In the shadows of the buildings the fall air felt wintry. He had not been down here in more years than he cared to remember.

The secretary, Miss Goode, greeted him warmly; she still remembered him from his days at Yale. Despite Prescott Bush's move to the Senate, they still kept his inner office for him, and as George stood outside the door he heard a piano. His father was singing. He had a wonderful singing voice, of which he was too proud.

George entered. Prescott Bush sat at an upright piano, playing Gilbert and Sullivan:

> *Go, ye heroes, go to glory*
> *Though you die in combat gory.*
> *Ye shall live in song and story.*
> *Go to immortality!*

Still playing, he glanced over his shoulder at George, then turned back and finished the verse:

Go to death, and go to slaughter;
Die, and every Cornish daughter
With her tears your grave shall water.
Go, ye heroes, go and die!

George was all too familiar with his father's theatricality. Six feet four inches tall, with thick salt-and-pepper hair and a handsome, craggy face, he carried off his Douglas Fairbanks imitation without any hint of self-consciousness. It was a quality George had tried to emulate his whole life.

Prescott adjusted the sheet music and swiveled his piano stool around. He waved at the sofa against the wall beneath his shelf of golfing trophies and photos of the Yale Glee Club. "Sit down, son. I'm glad you could make it. I know you must have a lot on your mind."

George remained standing. "What did you want to see me about?"

"Relax, George. This isn't the dentist's office."

"If it were, I would know what to expect."

"Well, one thing you can expect is to hear me tell you how proud I am."

"Proud? Did you see that game yesterday?"

Prescott Bush waved a hand. "Temporary setback. I'm sure you'll get them back this afternoon."

"Isn't it a little late for compliments?"

Prescott looked at him as calmly as if he were appraising some stock portfolio. His bushy eyebrows quirked a little higher. "George, I want you to sit down and shut up."

Despite himself, George sat. Prescott got up and paced to the window, looked down at the street, then started pacing again, his big hands knotted behind his back. George began to dread what was coming.

"George, I have been indulgent of you. Your entire life, despite my misgivings, I have treated you with kid gloves. You are not a stupid boy; at least your grades in school suggested you weren't. You've got that Phi Beta Kappa key, too—which only goes to show you what they are worth." He held himself very erect. "How old are you now?"

"Thirty-five."

Prescott shook his head. "Thirty-five? Lord. At *thirty-five* you show no more sense than you did at seventeen, when you told me that you intended to enlist in the navy. Despite the fact that the secretary of war himself, God-forbid-me *Franklin D. Roosevelt*'s secretary of war, had just told the graduating class that you, the cream of the nation's youth, could best serve your country by going to college instead of getting shot up on some Pacific island."

He strolled over to the piano, flipped pensively through the sheet music on top. "I remember saying to myself that day that maybe you knew something I didn't. You were young. I recalled my own recklessness in the first war. God knew we needed to lick the Japanese. But that didn't mean a boy of your parts and prospects should do the fighting. I prayed you'd survive and that by the time you came back you'd have grown some sense." Prescott closed the folder of music and faced him.

George, as he had many times before, instead of looking into his father's eyes looked at a point beyond his left ear. At the moment, just past that ear he could see half of a framed photograph of one of his father's singing groups. Probably the Silver Dollar

Quartet. He could not make out the face of the man on the end of the photo. Some notable businessman, no doubt. A man who sat on four boards of directors making decisions that could topple the economies of six banana republics while he went to the club to shoot eight-handicap golf. Someone like Prescott Bush.

"When you chose this baseball career," his father said, "I finally realized you had serious problems facing reality. I would think the dismal history of your involvement in this sport might have taught you something. Now, by the grace of God and sheer luck you find yourself, on the verge of your middle years, in the spotlight. I can't imagine how it happened. But I know one thing: you must take advantage of this situation. You must seize the brass ring before the carousel stops. As soon as the Series is over I want you to take up a career in politics."

George stopped looking at the photo. His father's eyes were on his. "Politics? But Dad, I thought I could become a coach."

"A coach?"

"A coach. I don't know anything about politics. I'm a baseball player. Nobody is going to elect a baseball player."

Prescott Bush stepped closer. He made a fist, beginning to be carried away by his own rhetoric. "Twenty years ago, maybe, you would be right. But George, times are changing. People want an attractive face. They want somebody famous. It doesn't matter so much what they've done before. Look at Eisenhower. He had no experience of government. The only reason he got elected was because he was a war hero. Now you're a war hero, or at least we can dress you up into a reasonable facsimile of one. You're Yale educated, a brainy boy. You've got breeding and class. You're not bad looking. And thanks to this children's game, you're famous—for the next two weeks, anyway. So after the Series we strike while the iron's hot. You retire from baseball. File for Congress on the Republican ticket in the third Connecticut district."

"But I don't even live in Connecticut."

"Don't be contrary, George. You're a baseball player; you live on the road. Your last stable residence before you took up this, this—baseball—was New Haven. I've held an apartment there for years in your name. That's good enough for the people we're going to convince."

His father towered over him. George got up, retreated toward the window. "But I don't know anything about politics!"

"So? You'll learn. Despite the fact I've been against your playing baseball, I have to say that it will work well for you. It's the national game. Every kid in the country wants to be a ballplayer. Most of the adults do, too. It's hard enough for people from our class to overcome the prejudice against money, George. Baseball gives you the common touch. Why, you'll probably be the only Republican in the Congress ever to have showered with a Negro. On a regular basis, I mean."

"I don't even like politics."

"George, there are only two kinds of people in the world: the employers and the employees. You were born and bred to the former. I will not allow you to persist in degrading yourself into one of the latter."

"Dad, really, I appreciate your trying to look out for me. Don't get me wrong, gratitude's my middle name. But I love baseball. There's some opportunities there, I think. Down in Chattanooga I made some friends. I think I can be a good coach, and eventually I'll wear a manager's uniform."

Prescott Bush stared at him. George remembered that look when he'd forgotten to tie off the sailboat one summer up in Kennebunkport. He began to wilt. Eventually his father shook his head. "It comes to me at last that you do not possess the wits that God gave a Newfoundland retriever."

George felt his face flush. He looked away. "You're just jealous because I did what you never had the guts to do. What about you and your golf? You, you—dilettante! I'm going to be a manager!"

"George, if I want to I can step into that outer office, pick up the telephone, and in fifteen minutes set in motion a chain of events that will guarantee you won't get a job mopping toilets in the clubhouse."

George retreated to the window. "You think you can run my life? You just want me to be another appendage of Senator Bush. Well, you can forget it! I'm not your boy anymore."

"You'd rather spend the rest of your life letting men like this Communist Castro make a fool of you?"

George caught himself before he could completely lose his temper. Feeling hopeless, he drummed his knuckles on the windowsill, staring down into the narrow street. Down below them brokers and bankers hustled from meeting to meeting trying to make a buck. He might have been one of them. Would his father have been any happier?

He turned. "Dad, try for once to understand. I've never been so alive as I've been for moments—just moments out of eleven years—on the ball field. It's truly American."

"I agree with you, George—it's as American as General Motors. Baseball is a product. You players are the assembly-line workers who make it. But you refuse to understand that, and that's your undoing. Time eats you up, and you end up in the dustbin, a wasted husk."

George felt the helpless fury again. "Dad, you've got to—"

"Are you going to tell me I *have* to do something, George?" Prescott Bush sat back down at the piano, tried a few notes. He peeked over his shoulder at George, unsmiling, and began again to sing:

> *Go and do your best endeavor,*
> *And before all links we sever,*
> *We will say farewell forever.*
> *Go to glory and the grave!*
>
> *For your foes are fierce and ruthless,*
> *False, unmerciful and truthless.*
> *Young and tender, old and toothless,*
> *All in vain their mercy crave.*

George stalked out of the room, through the secretary's office, and down the corridor toward the elevators. It was all he could do to keep from punching his fist through the mahogany paneling. He felt his pulse thrumming in his temples, slowing as he waited for the dilatory elevator to arrive, rage turning to depression.

Riding down he remembered something his mother had said to him twenty years before. He'd been one of the best tennis players at the River Club in Kennebunkport. One summer, in front of the whole family, he lost a championship match. He knew he'd let them down, and tried to explain to his mother that he'd only been off his game.

"George," she'd said, "you don't have a game."

The elevator let him out into the lobby. On Seventh Avenue he stepped into a bar and ordered a beer. On the TV in the corner, sound turned low, an announcer was going over the highlights of the Series. The TV switched to an image of some play in the field. George heard a reference to "Senator Bush," but he couldn't tell which one of them they were talking about.

10.

A few of the pitchers, including Camilo Pascual, the young right-hander who was to start game five, were the only others in the clubhouse when George showed up. The tone was grim. Nobody wanted to talk about how their season might be over in a few hours. Instead they talked fishing.

Pascual was nervous; George was keyed tighter than a Christmas toy. Ten years of obscurity, and now hero one day, goat the next. The memory of his teammates' hollow words of encouragement as he'd slumped back into the dugout each time Castro struck him out made George want to crawl into his locker and hide. The supercilious brown bastard. What kind of man would go out of his way to humiliate him?

Stobbs sauntered in, whistling. He crouched into a batting stance, swung an imaginary Louisville Slugger through Kralick's head, then watched it sail out into the imaginary bleachers. "Hey, guys, I got an idea," he said. "If we get the lead today, let's call time out."

But they didn't get the lead. By the top of the second, they were down 3–0. But Pascual, on the verge of being yanked, settled down. The score stayed frozen through six. The Senators finally got to Jones in the seventh when Allison doubled and Killebrew hit a towering home run into the bullpen in left center: 3–2, Giants. Meanwhile the Senators' shaky relief pitching held, as the Giants stranded runners in the sixth and eighth and hit into three double plays.

By the top of the ninth the Giants still clung to the 3–2 lead, three outs away from winning the Series, and the rowdy New York fans were gearing up for a celebration. The Senators' dugout was grim, but they had the heart of the order up: Sievers, Lemon, Killebrew. Among them they had hit ninety-four home runs that season. They had also struck out almost three hundred times.

Rigney went out to talk to Jones, then left him in, though he had Stu Miller up and throwing in the bullpen. Sievers took the first pitch for a strike, fouled off the second, and went down swinging at a high fastball. The crowd roared.

Lemon went into the hole 0–2, worked the count even, and grounded out to second.

The crowd, on their feet, chanted continuously now. Fans pounded on the dugout roof, and the din was deafening. Killebrew stepped into the batter's box, and George moved up to the on-deck circle. On one knee in the dirt, he bowed his head and prayed that Killer would get on base.

"He's praying!" Castro shouted from the Giants' dugout. "Well might you pray, Sen-a-tor Bush!"

Killebrew called time and spat toward the Giants. The crowd screamed abuse at him. He stepped back into the box. Jones went into his windup. Killebrew took a tremendous cut and missed. The next pitch was a changeup that Killebrew mistimed and slammed five hundred feet down the left-field line into the upper deck—foul. The crowd quieted. Jones stepped off the mound, wiped his brow, shook off a couple of signs, and threw another fastball that Killebrew slapped into right for a single.

That was it for Jones. Rigney called in Miller. Lavagetto came out and spoke to George. "All right. He won't try anything tricky. Look for the fastball."

George nodded, and Lavagetto bounced back into the dugout. "Come on, George Herbert Walker Bush!" Consolo yelled. George tried to ignore the crowd and the Giants' heckling while Miller warmed up. His stomach was tied into twelve knots. He avoided looking into the box seats where he knew his father sat. Politics. What the blazes did he want with politics?

Finally, Miller was ready. "Play ball!" the ump yelled. George stepped into the box.

He didn't wait. The first pitch was a fastball. He turned on it, made contact, but got too far under it. The ball soared out into left, a high, lazy fly. George slammed down his bat and, heart sinking, legged it out. The crowd cheered, and Alou circled back to make the catch. George was rounding first, his head down, when he heard a stunned groan from fifty thousand throats at once. He looked up to see Alou slam his glove to the ground. Miller, on the mound, did the same. The Senators' dugout was leaping insanity. Somehow, the ball had carried far enough to drop into the overhanging upper deck, 250 feet away. Home run. Senators lead, 4–3.

"Lucky bastard!" Castro shouted as Bush rounded third.

Stobbs shut them down in the ninth, and the Senators won.

11.

SENATOR BUSH SAVES WASHINGTON! the headlines screamed. MAKES CASTRO SEE RED. They were comparing it to the 1923 Series, held in these same Polo Grounds, where Casey Stengel, a thirty-two-year-old outfielder who'd spent twelve years in the majors without doing anything that might cause anyone to remember him, batted .417 and hit home runs to win two games.

Reporters stuck to him like flies on sugar. The pressure of released humiliation loosened George's tongue. "I know Castro's type," he said, snarling what he hoped was a good imitation of a manly snarl. "At the wedding he's the bride, at the funeral he's the dead person. You know, the corpse. That kind of poor sportsmanship just burns me up. But I've been around. He can't get my goat because of where I've got it in the guts department."

The papers ate it up. Smart money had said the Series would never go back to Washington. Now they were on the train to Griffith Stadium, and if the Senators were going to lose, at least the home fans would have the pleasure of going through the agony in person.

Game six was a slugfest. Five homers: McCovey, Mays, and Cepeda for the Giants; Naragon and Lemon for the Senators. Kaat and Antonelli were both knocked out early. The lead changed back and forth three times.

George hit three singles, a sacrifice fly, and drew a walk. He scored twice. The Senators came from behind to win, 10–8. In the ninth, George sprained his ankle sliding into third. It was all he could do to hobble into the locker room after the game.

"It doesn't hurt," George told the reporters. "Bar always says, and she knows me better than anybody, go ahead and ask around,

'You're the game one, George.' Not the gamy one, mind you!" He laughed, smiled a crooked smile.

"A man's gotta do what a man's gotta do," he told them. "That strong but silent type of thing. My father said so."

12.

Fonseca waited until Fidel emerged into the twilight outside the Fifth Street stadium exit. As Fonseca approached, his hand on the slick automatic in his overcoat pocket, his mind cast back to their political years in Havana, where young men such as they, determined to seek prominence, would be as likely to face the barrel of a pistol as an electoral challenge. Ah, nostalgia.

"Pretty funny, that Sen-a-TOR Bush," Fonseca said. He shoved Fidel back toward the exit. Nobody was around.

If Fidel was scared, a slight narrowing of his eyes was the only sign. "What is this about?"

"Not a thing. Raúl says hello."

"Hello to Raúl."

"Mirta says hello, too."

"You haven't spoken to her." Fidel took a cigar from his mohair jacket, fished a knife from a pocket, trimmed off the end, and lit it with a battered Zippo. "She doesn't speak with exiled radicals. Or mobsters."

Fonseca was impressed by the performance. "Are you going to do this job, finally?"

"I can only do my half. One cannot make a sow look like a ballet dancer."

"It is not apparent to our friends that you're doing your half."

"Tell them I am truly frightened, Luis." He blew a plume

of smoke. It was dark now, almost full night. "Meanwhile, I am hungry. Let me buy you a Washington dinner."

The attitude was all too typical of Fidel, and Fonseca was sick of it. He had fallen under Fidel's spell back in the university, thought him some sort of great man. In 1948 Fidel's self-regard could be justified as necessary boldness. But when the head of the National Sports Directory was shot dead in the street, Fonseca had not been the only one to think Fidel was the killer. It was a gesture of suicidal machismo of the sort that Fidel admired. Gunmen scoured the streets for them. While Fonseca hid in a series of airless apartments, Fidel got a quick tryout with the Giants, married Mirta, and abandoned Havana, leaving Fonseca and their friends to deal with the consequences.

"If you don't take care, Fidel, our friends will buy you a Washington grave."

"They are not my friends—or yours."

"No, they aren't. But this was our choice, and you have to go through with it." Fonseca watched a beat cop stop at the corner, then turn away down the street. He moved closer, stuck the pistol into Fidel's ribs. "You know, Fidel, I have a strong desire to shoot you right now. Who cares about the World Series? It would be pleasant just to see you bleed."

The tip of Fidel's cigar glowed in the dark. "This Bush would be no hero then."

"But I would be."

"You would be a traitor."

Fonseca laughed. "Don't say that word again. It evokes too many memories." He plucked the cigar from Fidel's hand, threw it onto the sidewalk. "Athletes should not smoke."

He pulled the gun back, drew his hand from his overcoat, and crossed the street.

13.

The night before, the Russians announced they had shot down a US spy plane over the Soviet Union. A pack of lies, President Nixon said. No such planes existed.

Meanwhile, on the clubhouse radio, a feverish announcer was discussing strategy for game seven. A flock of telegrams had arrived to urge the Senators on. Tacked on the bulletin board in the locker room, they gave pathetic glimpses into the hearts of the thousands who had for years tied their sense of well-being to the fate of a punk team like the Senators.

- *Show those racially polluted commie-symps what Americans stand for.*
- *My eight-year-old son, crippled by polio, sits up in his wheelchair so that he can watch the games on TV.*
- *Jesus Christ, creator of the heavens and earth, is with you.*

As George laced up his spikes over his aching ankle in preparation for the game, thinking about facing Castro one last time, it came to him that he was terrified.

In the last week he had entered an atmosphere he had not lived in since Yale. He was a hero. People had expectations of him. He was admired and courted. If he had received any respect before, it was the respect given to someone who refused to quit when every indication shouted he ought to try something else. He did not have the braggadocio of a Castro. Yet here, miraculously, he was shining.

Except he *knew* that Castro was better than he was, and he knew that anybody who really knew the game knew it, too. He knew that this week was a fluke, a strange conjunction of the stars that had knocked him into the "groove," as the old man in the bar had said. It could evaporate at any instant. It could already have evaporated.

Lavagetto and Mr. Griffith came in and turned off the radio. "Okay, boys," Lavagetto said. "People in this city been waiting a long time for this game. A lot of you been waiting your whole careers for it, and you younger ones might not get a lot of chances to play in the seventh game of the World Series. Nobody gave us a chance to be here today, but here we are. Let's make the most of it, go out there and kick the blazes out of them, then come back in and drink some champagne!"

The team whooped and headed out to the field.

Coming up the tunnel, the sound of cleats scraping damp concrete, the smell of stale beer and mildew, Bush could see a sliver of the bright grass and white baselines, the outfield fence and crowds in the bleachers, sunlight so bright it hurt his eyes. When the team climbed the dugout steps onto the field, a great roar rose from the throats of the thirty thousand fans. He had never heard anything so beautiful, or frightening. The concentrated focus of their hope swelled George's chest with unnamable emotion, brought tears to his eyes, and he ducked his head and slammed his fist into his worn first-baseman's glove.

The teams lined up on the first- and third-base lines for the National Anthem. The fans began cheering even before the last line of the song faded away, and George jogged to first, stepping on the bag for good luck. His ankle twinged; his whole leg felt hot. Ramos finished his warm-ups, the umpire yelled "Play ball!" and they began.

Ramos set the Giants down in order in the top of the first. In the home half Castro gave up a single to Allison, who advanced to third on a single by Lemon. Killebrew walked. Bush came up with bases loaded, one out. He managed a fly ball to right, and Allison beat the throw to the plate. Castro struck out Bertoia to end the inning. 1–0, Senators,

Ramos retired the Giants in order in the second. In the third, Lemon homered to make it 2–0.

Castro had terrific stuff, but seemed to be struggling with his control. Or else he was playing games again. By the fourth inning he had seven strike-outs to go along with the two runs he'd given up. He shook off pitch after pitch, and Schmidt went out to argue with him. Rigney talked to him in the dugout, and the big Cuban waved his arms as if emphatically arguing his case.

Schmidt homered for the Giants in the fourth, but Ramos was able to get out of the inning without further damage. Senators, 2–1.

In the bottom of the fourth, George came up with a man on first. Castro struck him out on a high fastball that George missed by a foot.

In the Giants' fifth, Spencer doubled off the wall in right. Alou singled him home to tie the game, and one out later Mays launched a triple over Allison's head into the deepest corner of center field, just shy of the crazy wall protecting Mrs. Mahan's backyard. Giants up, 3–2. The crowd groaned. As he walked out to the mound, Lavagetto was already calling for a left-hander to face McCovey. Ramos kicked the dirt, handed him the ball, and headed to the showers, and Stobbs came on to pitch to McCovey. He got McCovey on a grounder to George at first, and Davenport on a pop fly.

The Senators failed to score in the bottom of the fifth and sixth, but in the seventh, George, limping for real now, doubled in Killer to tie the game, and was driven home, wincing as he forced weight down on his ankle, on a single by Naragon. Senators 4–3. The crowd roared.

Rigney came out to talk to Castro, but Castro convinced him to let him stay in. He'd struck out twelve already, and the Giants' bullpen was depleted after the free-for-all in game six.

The score stayed that way through the eighth. By the top of the ninth the crowd was going wild in the expectation of a world championship. Lavagetto had pulled Stobbs, who sat next to Bush in his warm-up jacket, and put in the right-hander Hyde, who'd led the team in saves.

The Giants mounted another rally. On the first pitch, Spencer laid a bunt down the first-base line. Hyde stumbled coming off the mound, and George, taken completely by surprise, couldn't get to it on his bad foot. He got up limping, and the trainer came out to ask him if he could play. George was damned if he would let it end so pitifully, and shook him off. Alou grounded to first, Spencer advancing. Cepeda battled the count full, then walked.

Mays stepped into the box. Hyde picked up the rosin bag, walked off the mound, and rubbed up the ball. George could see he was sweating. Hyde stepped back onto the rubber, took the sign, and threw a high fastball that Mays hit four hundred feet, high into the bleachers in left. The Giants leapt out of the dugout, slapping Mays on the back, congratulating each other. The fans tore their clothing in despair, slumped into their seats, cursed and moaned. The proper order had been restored to the universe. George looked over at Castro, who sat in the dugout impassively. Lavagetto came out to talk to Hyde. The crowd booed when the manager left him in, but Hyde managed to get them out of the inning without further damage. As the Senators left the field the organist tried to stir the crowd, but despair had settled over them like a lead blanket. Giants, 6–4.

In the dugout Lavagetto tried to get them up for the inning. "This is it, gentlemen. Time to prove we belong here."

Allison had his bat out and was ready to go to work before the umpire had finished sweeping off the plate. Castro threw three warm-ups and waved him into the box. When Allison lined a single between short and third, the crowd cheered and rose to their feet. Sievers, swinging for the fences, hit a nubbler to the mound, a sure double play. Castro pounced on it in good time, but fumbled the ball, double-clutched, and settled for the out at first. The fans cheered.

Rigney came out to talk it over. He and Schmidt stayed on the mound a long time, Castro gesturing wildly, insisting he wasn't tired. He had struck out the side in the eighth.

Rigney left him in, and Castro rewarded him by striking out Lemon for his seventeenth of the game, a new World Series record. Two down. Killebrew was up. The fans hovered on the brink of nervous collapse. The Senators were torturing them; they were going to drag this out to the last fatal out, not give them a clean killing or a swan-dive fade—no, they would hold out the chance of victory to the last moment, then crush them dead.

Castro rubbed up the ball, checked Allison over his shoulder, shook off a couple of Schmidt's signs, and threw. He got Killebrew in an 0–2 hole, then threw four straight balls to walk him. The crowd noise reached a frenzy.

And so, as he stepped to the plate in the bottom of the ninth, two outs, George Herbert Walker Bush represented the winning run, the potential end to twenty-seven years of Washington frustration, the apotheosis of his life in baseball, or the ignominious end of it. Castro had him set up again, to be the glorious goat for the entire Series. His ankle throbbed. "C'mon, Senator!" Lavagetto shouted. "Make me a genius!"

Castro leaned forward, shook off Schmidt's call, shook off another. He went into his windup, then paused, ball hidden in his glove, staring soberly at George—not mocking, not angry, certainly not intimidated—as if he were looking down from a reconnaissance plane flying high above the ballpark. George tried not to imagine what he was thinking.

Then Castro lifted his knee, strode forward, and threw a fat hanging curve, the sweetest, dopiest, laziest pitch he had thrown all day. George swung. As he did, he felt the last remaining strength of the dying Babe Ruth course down his arms. The ball kissed off the sweet spot of the bat and soared, pure and white as a six-year-old's prayer, into the left-field bleachers.

The stands exploded. Fans boiled onto the field even before George touched second. Allison did a kind of hopping balletic dance around the bases ahead of him, a cross between Nureyev and a man on a pogo stick. The Senators ran out of the dugout and bear-hugged George as he staggered around third; like a broken-field runner he struggled through the fans toward home. A weeping fat man in a plaid shirt, face contorted by ecstasy, blocked his way to the plate, and it was all he could do to keep from knocking him over.

As his teammates pulled him toward the dugout, he caught a glimpse over his shoulder of the Franchise standing on the mound, watching the melee and George at the center of it with an inscrutable expression on his face. Then George was pulled back into the maelstrom and surrendered to his bemused joy.

14.

Long after everyone had left and the clubhouse was deserted, Fidel dressed, and instead of leaving walked back out to the field. The stadium was dark, but in the light of the moon he could make out the trampled infield and the obliterated base paths. He stood on the mound and looked around at the empty stands. He was about to leave when someone called him from the dugout. "Beautiful, isn't it?"

Fidel approached. It was a thin man in his sixties. He wore a sporty coat and a white dress shirt open at the collar. "Yes?" Fidel asked.

"The field is beautiful."

Fidel sat next to him on the bench. They stared across the diamond. The wind rustled the trees beyond the outfield walls. "Some people think so," Fidel said.

"I thought we might have a talk," the man said. "I've been waiting around the ballpark before the last few games trying to get hold of you."

"I don't think we have anything to talk about, Mr. . . ."

"Weaver. Buck Weaver."

"Mr. Weaver. I don't know you, and you don't know me."

The man came close to smiling. "I know about winning the World Series. And losing it. I was on the winning team in 1917, and the losing one in 1919."

"You would not be kidding me, old man?"

"No. For a long time after the second one, I couldn't face a ballpark. Especially during the Series. I might have gone to quite a few, but I couldn't make myself do it. Now I go to the games every chance I get."

"You still enjoy baseball."

"I love the game. It reminds me where my body is buried." As he said all of this the man kept smiling, as if it were a funny story he was telling, and a punch line waited in the near future.

"You should quit teasing me, old man," Fidel said. "You're still alive."

"To all outward indications I'm alive, most of the year now. For a long time I was dead the year round. Eventually I was dead only during the summer, and now it's come down to just the Series."

"You are the mysterious one. Why do you not simply tell me what you want with me?"

"I want to know why you did what you just did."

"What did I do?"

"You threw the game."

Fidel watched him. "You cannot prove that."

"I don't have to prove it. I know it, though."

"How do you know it?"

"Because I've seen it done before."

From somewhere in his boyhood, Fidel recalled the name

now. Buck Weaver. The 1919 Series. "The Black Sox. You were one of them."

That appeared to be the punch line. The man's smile faded. His eyes were set in painful nets of wrinkles. "I was never one of them. But I knew about it, and that was enough for that bastard Landis to kick me out of the game."

"What does that have to do with me?"

"At first I wanted to stop you. Now I just want to know why you did it. Are you so blind to what you've got that you could throw it away? You're not a fool. Why?"

"I have my reasons, old man. Eighty thousand dollars, for one."

"You don't need the money."

"My brother, in prison, does. The people in my home do."

"Don't give me that. You don't really care about them."

Fidel let the moment stretch, listening to the rustling of the wind through the trees, the traffic in the distant street. "No? Well, perhaps. Perhaps I did it just because I *could*. Because the game betrayed me, because I wanted to show it is as corrupt as the *mierda* around it. It's not any different from the world. You know how it works. How every team has two black ballplayers—the star and the star's roommate." He laughed. "It's not a religion, and this place"—he gestured at Griffith Stadium looming in the night before them—"is not a cathedral."

"I thought that way, when I was angry," Weaver said. "I was a young man. I didn't know how much it meant to me until they took it away."

"Old man, you would have lost it regardless. How old were you? Twenty-five? Thirty? In ten years it would have been taken from you anyway, and you'd be in the same place you are now."

"But I'd have my honor. I wouldn't be a disgrace."

"That's only what other people say. Why should you let their ignorance affect who you are?"

"Brave words. But I've lived it. You haven't—yet." Plainly upset, Weaver walked out onto the field to stand at third base. He crouched; he looked in toward the plate. After a while he straightened, a frail old man, and called in toward Fidel: "When I was twenty-five, I stood out here; I thought I had hold of a baseball in my hand. It turned out it had hold of me."

He came back and stood at the top of the dugout steps. "Don't worry, I'm not going to tell. I didn't then, and I won't now."

Weaver left, and Fidel sat in the dugout.

15.

They used the photo of George's painfully shy, crooked smile, a photograph taken in the locker room after he'd been named MVP of the 1959 World Series, on his first campaign poster.

In front of the photographers and reporters, George was greeted by Mr. Griffith. And his father. Prescott Bush wore a political smile as broad as his experience of what was necessary to impress the world. He put his arm around his son's shoulders, and although George was a tall man, his father was still a taller one.

"I'm proud of you, son," Prescott said, in a voice loud enough to be heard by everyone. "You've shown the power of decency and persistence in the face of hollow boasts."

Guys were spraying champagne, running around with their hair sticky and their shirts off, whooping and shouting and slapping each other on the back. Even his father's presence couldn't entirely deflect George's satisfaction. He had done it. Proved himself for once and for all. He wished Bar and the boys could be there. He wanted to shout in the streets, to stay up all night, be pursued by beautiful women. He sat in front of his locker and patiently answered the reporters' questions at length, repeatedly. Only gradually did the furor settle down. George glanced across the room to the brightly lit corner where Prescott was talking, on camera, with a television reporter.

It was clear that his father was setting him up for this planned political career. It infuriated him that he assumed he could control George so easily, but at the same time George felt confused about what he really wanted for himself. As he sat there in the diminishing chaos, Lavagetto came over and sat down beside him. The manager was still high from the victory.

"I don't believe it!" Lavagetto said. "I thought he was crazy, but old Tricky Dick must have known something I didn't!"

"What do you mean?"

"Mean?—nothing. Just that the president called after the first game and told me to bat you behind Killebrew. I thought he was crazy. But it paid off."

George remembered Prescott Bush whispering into Nixon's ear. He felt a crushing weight on his chest. He stared over at his father in the TV lights, not hearing Lavagetto.

But as he watched, he wondered. If his father had indeed fixed the Series, then everything George had accomplished came to nothing. But his father was an honorable man. Besides, Nixon was noted for his sports obsession, full of fantasies because he himself was a poor athlete. His calling Lavagetto was the kind of thing he would do anyway. Winning had been too hard for it to be a setup. No, Castro had wanted to humiliate George, and George had stood up to him.

The reporter finished talking to his father; the TV lights snapped off. George thanked Lavagetto for the faith the manager had shown in him, and limped over to Prescott Bush.

"Feeling pretty good, George?"

"It was a miracle we won. I played above myself."

"Now, don't take what I said back in New York so much to heart. You proved yourself equal to the challenge, that's all." Prescott lowered his voice. "Have you thought any more about the proposition I put to you?"

George looked his father in the eye. If Prescott Bush felt any discomfort, there was no trace of it in his patrician's gaze.

"I guess maybe I've played enough baseball," George said.

His father put his hand on George's shoulder; it felt like a burden. George shrugged it off and headed for the showers.

Many years later, as he faced the Washington press corps in the East Room of the White House, George Herbert Walker Bush was to remember that distant afternoon, in the ninth inning of the seventh game of the World Series, when he'd stood in the batter's box against the Franchise. He had not known then what he now understood: that, like his father, he would do anything to win.

Imagining the Human Future: Up, Down, or Sideways

A lecture I gave at a conference, Imagining
the Human Future, sponsored by the
National Academy of Sciences, at Chicago's
Field Museum in November 2001.

I am a science fiction writer, and a professor of American literature. As an undergraduate I was an astrophysics major who discovered, to my chagrin, that tensor calculus was not my friend, and to my surprise, that my talents did not lie in the sciences as much as in the humanities. Yet the subjects of this conference have been the center of my interest since I was a teenager. I am honored to have been invited to speak to you, and only hope I have something to say that may prove worthwhile after all that has been put before you in the last three days.

I am going to talk a bit about science fiction's vision of the posthuman condition, and especially about its ethical implications. I intend to get at this by telling you about some books.

At North Carolina State University I teach a course in the history and development of science fiction. This semester I assigned some works by H.G. Wells and W. Olaf Stapledon, and I'd like to begin by exploring what those two writers had to say about the human future.

It strikes me that you might have done better to invite H.G. Wells to speak to you today—but I understand that, unfortunately, he is otherwise engaged. Wells spent his entire public career and much of his private life speculating about the human future, and his writing laid the foundation for much of what science fiction has had to say on this subject in the last one hundred years. As a young man, he studied biology under Darwin's disciple and defender Thomas Henry Huxley, and the vision of evolution that was opened to him at that time informed everything he wrote for the rest of his life.

This semester my students read Wells's second science fiction novel, *The Island of Doctor Moreau*, published in 1896. In connection with that I read his last book, a brief essay entitled *Mind at the End of Its Tether*, published in 1945, a year before Wells's death.

These two works demonstrate that, beginning and end, Wells questioned the viability of humanity, and its ability to sustain a human culture.

Moreau is an evolutionary parable. Dr. Moreau is a vivisectionist, kicked out of England and set up on a South Seas island. There he attempts to turn animals into human beings. It is, if you will excuse the pun, a grisly business. None of his projects achieve more than a parody of humanity, and Moreau discards his failures on the island to fend for themselves. In order to curb the instincts of these Beast People, he gives them the "Law," which they struggle to follow against the pressure of their evolutionary natures: "Not to walk on all fours. Not to tear the bark of trees. Not to eat flesh." Periodically Moreau shows up to punish the violators, but otherwise he abandons them.

In later years Wells called *Moreau* "an exercise in youthful blasphemy," and it's easy to see why. Of course, *we* are the beast people. Moreau is a neglectful God. Wells saw humans as slightly evolved apes, with the beast lying very shallowly beneath our social surface. God may have given us the Ten Commandments, the *Tao Te Ching*, the Golden Rule, and the *Koran*, but we cannot maintain "the Law" in the face of our destructive instincts. In the novel's Gulliver-like ending, the castaway Edward Prendick returns to London but can't escape his vision of humans as animals prowling the city streets or gibbering from the pulpits.

After writing this bitterly skeptical book, Wells went on to spend most of his life advocating social change and scientific education. If human civilization as it existed in 1896 was inadequate, Wells thought we might reach a state of posthumanity by social reorganization and scientific understanding. One of his most famous quotes is "Human history becomes more and more a race between education and catastrophe." He bet his creative life on the hope that education could advance humanity to a utopian stage of existence—we had the means, if we could only muster the will. He did not believe in a God of theology: he titled his 1922 utopia *Men Like Gods*.

I think it is pretty clear that by the end of his life, Wells thought his bet had failed. Written in the wake of World War II, *Mind at the End of Its Tether* is a despairing summation. Wells can no longer see the future. Like Prendick at the end of *Moreau*, he finds himself living among the Beast People and concludes that humanity is doomed unless it makes an evolutionary leap. Even then we will be displaced.

> A series of events has forced upon the intelligent observer the realisation that the human story has already

come to an end and that *Homo sapiens*, as he has been pleased to call himself, is in his present form played out. The stars in their courses have turned against him and he has to give place to some other animal better adapted to face the fate that closes in more and more swiftly upon mankind.

That new animal may be an entirely alien strain, or it may arise as a new modification of the *hominidae*, and even as a direct continuation of the human phylum, but it will certainly not be human. . . .

Man must go steeply up or down and the odds seem to be all in favour of his going down and out. If he goes up, then so great is the adaptation demanded of him that he must cease to be a man. Ordinary man is at the end of his tether. Only a small, highly adaptable minority of the species can possibly survive.

It is important to note that Wells believes humans face this crisis, not because they lack material power, but because of the inability of "hard imaginative thinking . . . to keep pace with the expansion and complication of human societies and organizations." In 1945, Wells longs, not for any increase in human power to control nature, but for what I might call an *ethical* posthumanity.

(I might add that this longing was implicit in his work from the beginning. In his 1906 novel *In the Days of the Comet*, he proposes the Earth passing through a tail of a comet that chemically transforms the human psyche. His hero, as the earth passes into the comet's tail, is pursuing his lover who deserted him, revolver in his hand and murder in his heart. He passes out. When he wakes in the morning, he, his lover, and his rival form a threesome. *Men Like Gods*, indeed.)

In what way might our descendants go up or down? For that, we get a clearer picture in Wells's successor and contemporary, W. Olaf Stapledon. Stapledon's peculiar fiction is everywhere informed by the concern for the evolutionary fate of humanity so evident in Wells. When asked why he had not acknowledged the influence of Wells on his 1930 book *Last and First Men*, Stapledon wrote, "A man does not record his debt to the air he breathes."

Last and First Men tells the history of the human race from 1930 until two billion years in the future. Over eons humanity evolves through seventeen successive forms, culminating in the Last Men, hardly human at all, living on Neptune. In the early stages of this saga Stapledon speculates on a great number of changes that seem still relevant today: the Americanization of the planet, the possibility of the annihilation of humanity by accident or political madness, the disasters that could take place when oil resources are depleted, the challenges and risks of genetic engineering, the spiritual folly of an obsession with youth, the development of artificial intelligence.

In *Last and First Men* (and in his later, even more stunning speculation, *Star Maker*), Stapledon envisions a human future of ceaseless evolutionary change and adaptation, guided by a spiritual striving for mutual understanding between individuals, and for oneness with the universe. He looks down on the human race with a chilly detachment, from which the tragedies and achievements of a millennium shrink to next to nothing. As he says in *Star Maker*, "It is enough to have been created, to have embodied for a moment the infinite and tumultuously creative spirit. It is infinitely more than enough to have been used."

This is cold comfort to those of us animalcules experiencing our brief moment of time, watching Tom Brokaw and *Friends*, and worrying about the future. It's bracing to realize that Brokaw and *Friends* are not the apex of the human story, but the equanimity with which Stapledon contemplates an extinction that seems even more likely today than it did in the 1930s is difficult to maintain.

In his 1935 novel *Odd John*, Stapledon brings posthumanism closer to home and shows its ethical implications in more immediate terms.

Odd John imagines our immediate successor. John is an evolutionary advance, the next stage in human development. Morally, he is beyond us. The story is told from the point of view of an adult who serves as John's confidant and servant, known only by John's affectionate and contemptuous nickname for him, "Fido"—a fair indication of John's attitude toward *Homo sapiens*.

John has his sympathies for us, but they are remote ones. At the age of nine, he deliberately kills a policeman who catches him in a petty burglary. He compares it to the time he had to kill a tame mouse because the maids did not like it running around the house. He even contemplates killing the policeman's wife as an act of charity, in order to save her the grief that would come to her upon the loss of her husband. When the interests of *Homo superior* and those of *Homo sapiens* come into conflict, John manipulates and discards human beings—yet he is as vulnerable, in his way, as you and I, and something other than a villain.

Odd John raises the question of what moral obligations our successors should have toward us. Since then, the question has been pursued in numerous works of science fiction. In the last twenty years, as technology and biology have made the prospect of a posthuman race more of a possibility than a speculation, many science fiction writers have weighed in. In William Gibson's work, artificial intelligences end up running the world, and human beings (some of us at least) find refuge as data inside computers. The Australian writer Greg Egan has pursued various visions of humanity as computer information. Greg Bear has written several novels about the human genotype being superseded through biotechnology.

The result of these speculations is a menu of visions:

Male and female are fundamentally changed. The male no longer rules. The distinctions between the sexes, biological and cultural, have become fluid or no longer exist.

Our descendants create cultural enclaves. They evolve in clades. They are possessed by ideas. They use language differently.

Through nanotechnology, their dominion over the material world reaches miraculous levels.

They do not think as we do. They have an altered limbic system. They are autistic. They have no fixed personalities. They think in other directions. Their minds are technically augmented. Their memories enhanced. Their sensory abilities expanded. They have no bodies at all. They are data in computers, living in artificial environments.

They live hundreds of years. They do not die at all, unless voluntarily.

One of the most thoughtful of current science fiction writers, Vernor Vinge, author of the 1990s novels *A Fire upon the Deep* and *A Deepness in the Sky* published a provocative essay in 1993 that sums up much of science fiction's speculation about these changes.[*] The best way to summarize Vinge's paper is to quote its simple and daunting abstract: "Within thirty years, we will have the technological means to create superhuman intelligence. Shortly after, the human era will be ended."

Vinge coined the term "the Singularity" to describe this evolutionary leap that waits in our near future. Unfortunately, by its very nature, Vinge says, we cannot see past the Singularity. We cannot imagine what our successors' world will be like, we only know that the result will be a sudden and even catastrophic acceleration of "progress." Vinge accepts Wells's challenge of "up or out" and suggests that the answer is up.

Vinge does not define what he means by progress. Does he measure progress by technological advance? Increased scientific knowledge? Material power? That's the problem with much of SF's speculation—it says little or nothing about the ethics of posthumanism, when in fact that is the question that is *most* essential to us. To be fair, Vinge does briefly raise the ethical question and propose some standards. For instance, he quotes the appropriately named I.J. Good's "Meta Golden Rule" as a guide for posthumans: "Treat your inferiors as you would be treated by your superiors."[†]

I like that, but I feel there is more to be asked. To paraphrase that famous exchange between Mohandas Gandhi and a western reporter:

---

[*] Vernor Vinge, "The Coming Technological Singularity: How to Survive in the Post-human Era," San Diego State University, 1993, https://edoras.sdsu.edu/~vinge/misc/singularity.html.

[†] It turns out that this precept was originated not by I.J. Good but by the Roman statesman and philosopher Seneca.

Reporter: Mr. Gandhi, what do you think of posthuman civilization?

Gandhi: I think it would be a very good idea.

So do I, Mr. Gandhi. So here's my question: the day after I walk out of the clinic with a life expectancy of four hundred years and an IQ of 350, able effortlessly to do the tensor calculus that would have made me an astrophysicist instead of a lecturer on H.G. Wells, am I no longer human? How? In what way do my ethics differ? Have I gone from Republican to Democrat or, heaven forbid, vice versa? Do I still like professional football? Do I find the Marx Brothers funnier or less funny? Do I care more or less about what happens to migrant farm workers? To my cousin? To my daughter?

Moral posthumanism may come along with immortality, or computer augmentation of the human brain, or genetic alterations of the human genome, or Artificial Intelligence—it may even be a *product* of some of those things. But it is essentially apart from them. And, as I am about to suggest, it's not as if we haven't seen it already.

To imagine what the moral landscape of posthumanity might be, I'd like to cite a scene from one last work, Bruce Sterling's 1996 novel *Holy Fire*. In this book, power lies in the hands of conservative senior citizens who have managed their health and capital investments with equal care, gaining access to the latest advancements in life-extension technology, so at ninety they look fifty (but are *not* fifty). The penultimate chapter describes a meeting between the heroine Maya, and Helene, a police agent whose job it is to monitor the bohemian avant-garde, young people who are disaffected by this future society dominated by the prudent and the old. Maya herself is a ninety-four-year-old woman who has been rejuvenated to be physically twenty, with serious emotional and psychological consequences. (She isn't really twenty; she is ninety-four-going-on-twenty, a new kind of human neither old nor truly young.)

Maya has run away from her respectable life, and Helene, her contemporary, takes her to task for this. Helene reminds Maya how irresponsibility with technological resources has in the past has led to immense disasters. In the middle of the conversation, a real twenty-year-old, Natalie, rushes into their meeting. Natalie climbs out onto a window ledge and jumps to her death. Both Helene and Maya are shocked.

"I can't bear to look," Helene said, and shuddered. "I've seen this so many times . . . They just do it. They take possession of themselves and end their lives. It's an act of tremendous will."

"You should have let me go out there after her." [Maya says]

Helene shut the window with a bang. "You are in my charge, you are under arrest. You are not going anywhere, and you are not killing yourself. Sit down."

Plato rose and began to bark. Helene caught at his collar. "Poor things," she said, and wiped her eyes. "We have to let them go. There is no choice . . . Poor things, they are only human beings."

Maya slapped her face.

Helene looked at her in shocked surprise, then, slowly, turned her other cheek. "Do you feel better now, darling? Try the other one."

This passage in its moral complexity sums up something about the posthuman condition.

Why does Maya slap Helene? Maya feels Helene is inhuman in her acceptance of Natalie's suicide. Young people, in this world controlled by the nascent immortals and proto-posthumans, have little chance to make a difference. Maya feels Helene is responsible for pushing girls like Natalie into suicide. Her slap is a rebuke to the cool detachment of the posthuman Helene. Maya represents us, humans with twentieth-century hearts, who strike out at others out of our feeling of injustice, or abuse, or conviction. It's what we today would call "justifiable violence."

Helene turns the other cheek. I can't tell you how much, as a writer and literature professor, this move delights me. To have Helene do this is a brilliant stroke by Sterling, calling forth as it does our associations with the deepest mythic roots of Western Christian culture.

Turning the other cheek is something human beings have had the freedom to do throughout our evolutionary history—indeed, we celebrate the human who first admonished us to do so. In the context of this talk, we can recognize Jesus as the archetypal posthuman, not just Wells's man like a god but, as the story goes, a man who *was* God. We haven't found it easy to follow his example. Probably because we are not gods but only evolved hominids—that is, human beings.

Helene was born a human being. But she has lived long enough, and undergone enough changes through technology and a culture based on that technology, to have become something new. She even conceives of herself as something new—thus her pity for poor Natalie, the "human being" she looks down on. That pity sparks Maya's rage. It's not that Maya's blow doesn't cause an emotional reaction in Helene. She is shocked, and it takes her a moment to turn that cheek, but in the end she does. Presumably it is easier for Helene than for us to do so.

Like so many of science fiction's speculations about the future, I take the Singularity to be more a metaphor than a likely reality. But I would like to suggest (and I fervently hope) that if—as a result of our conscious efforts to understand and even change our intellect, neurology, biology, culture—there is indeed to be a Vingean Singularity, then in that posthuman world an act such as Helene's will be easier. I hope that our successors, be they biological or other, will find it *natural* to turn the other cheek.

This has little to do with intellect. And it's not a sentimental act. It partakes of some of the chilling coldness of Stapledon's Odd John, and his attitude toward the dead policeman's wife. Helene turns the other cheek because, in the complex and dangerous world that technology has bequeathed her, to do so is survival behavior. To Maya—who is, after all, the hero of the book—Helene is too ready to write off Natalie, too rational to be truly human. To paraphrase Wells, in Helene, "hard imaginative thinking *has* increased so as to keep pace with the expansion and complication of human societies and organizations." Helene does what Jesus does, and the context of the story shows us how inhuman an act Jesus' was. It is neither up nor down, but *sideways* of normal morality.

What this scene also implies is that we've already seen posthuman ethics. Most of us, in our own lives, at one time or another, have practiced them. We just can't stay at the posthuman level very long, any more that a person jumping up into the air can suspend himself at the apex of his leap. But with technology, we can fly, and perhaps our descendants will. It won't come simply through education, as Wells hoped. Something more fundamental must change.

Can we alter the human psyche? Should we? Must we?

Holy Fire ends with a visit by Maya to her husband Daniel, whom she has not seen for thirty or forty years. He is living in a cabin in the wilderness in Idaho. He has become an ancient squat apelike man who spends his days husbanding the land, using both muscle and high technology. He tells her of a plan to seed the atmosphere with fungus, spores that will repair the damages done by several centuries of industrialism. Maya questions the radical nature of this scheme. Daniel replies:

> "It's a response. New monster versus old monstrosity. We are as gods, Mia. We might as well get good at it " . . .
>
> He was a god, she decided. He hadn't been a god when he'd been with her. He'd been a man then, a good man. He wasn't a man any longer. Daniel was a very primitive god. A very small-scale god. A primitive steam-engine god. An amphibian god dutifully slogging mud for some coming race of reptiles.

And you and I, here in Chicago on November 3, 2001, as the world struggles to deal with age-old hostilities that threaten new destruction, thanks to the power of our inventions—we're fish, swimming in the shoals, unable as yet to breathe the air of the land where we must live in order to survive.

Thank you and good afternoon.

The President's Channel

HOWARD AWOKE IN THE middle of the night and could not go back to sleep. He looked at the bedside clock. 3:20. Jeanine lay solidly asleep beside him. After tossing and turning for a half hour, envying his wife her equanimity, he got out of bed and headed for the kitchen.

He rummaged through the pantry until he found a bag of chocolate chip cookies, poured himself a glass of milk and sat down at the table in the dark. The moonlight corning through the skylight softly illuminated the piles of bills at the corner of the table. He could make out the top one: $1,100 for the monthly auto premium. The premiums had leaped up back in January when Holly had taken some automatic weapons fire from a van driver on the beltline.

She was too young—only nine—to be driving, but she needed the after-school job if she was ever going to save up enough money to afford college. But she seemed more interested in boys; lately she'd taken to wearing fishnet stockings, and had shaved her eyebrows off and drawn them on a half Inch higher on her forehead. Howard blamed the sexy advertising from the companies that sponsored the third grade.

He finished the last of the cookies without even realizing it. They had gone down as tasteless as silicone. Jesus—the company urine test was tomorrow! He turned the bag over to the list of ingredients, and squinted to read them in the faint light. DERACINATED SUGAR, PROCESSED RICE FLOUR, DRIED BEET PULP, POTASSIUM CHLORIDE, PARTIALLY HYDROGENATED VEGETABLE SHORTENING, CALCIUM PROPIONATE, XANTHAN GUM, ARTIFICIAL COCOA SUBSTITUTE, INERT SYNTHETIC BULK MATERIALS NOT MORE THAN 30%.

He supposed there was nothing there to set off any alarms. He drained his glass of milk. It tasted like water—Jeanine insisted on buying only ultraskim. She acted as if somehow, if she managed everything precisely, she would keep them alive forever.

The only way to live forever was to be rich. The problem was, in order to build up anywhere near the vast sum it would take to have his genes recapped, they would have to live like paupers. Or he could raid Holly's college fund. Maybe Holly would do well enough in school to get some kind of scholarship? Right. The last time he had dialed up her academic record, she was maintaining only a B+ average. Eighty percent of the kids in school had a B+ average. Kids who showed up in class twice a week and spent the other days hitting themselves in the head with hammers carried B+ averages. Holly was more interested in getting her ears lopped than in school.

She could get corporate backing. But indenturing his daughter to a multinational was not a hurdle he was ready to make himself leap. Yet. He still felt pretty good. As long as he could keep his job.

Maybe they could win the lottery.

At this rate he would never get to sleep. He shuffled into the den and turned on the TV. The forty-six-inch screen lit and he flicked through the channels. Sportsnet was rerunning round sixteen of the perpetual NCAA Basketball Tournament. The Rage Channel had videos of people driving their cars off cliffs. He skipped past Sex Over Eighty to a gab channel.

The Wowsers were complaining about increasing wirehead addiction. Trying to get a constitutional amendment against electricity.

Elizabeth Taylor was getting married again.

Congressman Grieve was calling for an investigation of the administration, claiming that NSA operatives were feeding made-up footage into government monitors to cover up their crimes.

The Commentary All-Stars dismissed the president's nonex-istent sex life and brought on an oral hygienist, who critiqued the chief exec's spotty flossing and speculated what effect periodontal surgery might have on the upcoming budget negotiations.

Howard flipped around until he hit The President's Channel. The screen showed an image of a hallway; Howard recognized it as the one outside the President's bedroom. It was four a.m., and President Richter was awake.

Howard wondered what had gotten the Pres up in the middle of the night. Some government crisis? His latest poll numbers? A guilty conscience? The Pres was humming a song, the tune of which was familiar, but Howard couldn't make it out. The President liked to hum to himself; that was one of the first things Howard had noticed back when Richter was promoted from Vice Pres and had the camera and mic surgically implanted in his head.

His predecessor Gerringer had snapped midway through his second term—gone on a month-long binge, betting campaign money on football games, feeling up the interns, mainlining speedballs. So Richter found himself in a job he had never signed up for. So far he had seemed a completely stolid nonentity, a punching bag for the opposition, a vending machine for the lobbyists. Deposit your coins and receive your treat. Gerringer had been edgy; Richter was plain dull. Ratings on his channel had plunged. For all Howard knew, he might be the only person in the country tuning in at this late hour.

The Pres moved through the executive living quarters, down a hall and some back stairs. As he descended the stairs, Howard noted his clothing: he was wearing a wine-red robe and slippers. At the bottom of the stairs, the Pres poked his head around the corner, revealing a long view of a carpeted hall. A secret service man in a dark suit was stationed at the end of the corridor; the Pres jerked his head back, causing the image to spin dizzily.

Looked like Richter was finally going to do something interesting. Was he heading for some secret meeting? Maybe he had a rendezvous with his secretary, that Ms. Hodges? She wore short skirts and had long legs.

The image of the hallway bounced as the Pres dashed across the corridor, though a swinging door to a dark room. He flipped on the light.

It was a kitchen. The Pres moved directly over to a stainless-steel industrial refrigerator and took out a wheel of camembert. From a cupboard he took a box of crackers, a bottle of red wine, a bag of tortilla chips, a box of graham crackers, three chocolate bars, and a bag of marshmallows. He cleared a spot on a stainless steel table, pulled up a stool, and began gorging himself.

Howard watched for another fifteen minutes while the Pres put down half of the cheese, most of the wine, all of the chips. Watching the man raise the food toward the camera was like having food shoved at Howard through the television. By the time the Pres's hands were sticky with melted chocolate and marshmallows from the s'mores, Howard was feeling sleepy.

Pathetic bastard. No way he was going to get reelected.

Howard turned off the TV. He looked in on Holly, who lay sleeping, her face scrubbed free of paint, her scowl relaxed, looking more like a nine-year-old than she ever did when she was awake. He pulled the covers up over her sprawl and shuffled back to the bedroom.

Jeanine stirred. "Are you okay?"

Howard kissed her on the forehead. "Compared to what?"

The Last American

The Life of Andrew Steele
Recreated by Fiona 13

Reviewed by The Old Guy

> "I don't blame my father for beating me. I don't blame
> him for tearing the book I was reading from my hands,
> and I don't blame him for locking me in the basement.
> When I was a child, I did blame him. I was angry,
> and I hated my father. But as I grew older I came to
> understand that he did what was right for me, and now
> I look upon him with respect and love, the respect and
> love he always deserved, but that I was unable to give
> him because I was too young and self-centered."
>
> —Andrew Steele, 2077
> Conversation with Hagiographer

During the thirty-three years Andrew Steele occupied the Oval
Office of what was then called the White House, in what was then
called the United States of America (not to be confused with the
current United State of Americans), on the corner of his desk he
kept an antiquated device of the early twenty-first century called

a taser. Typically used by law enforcement officers, it functioned by shooting out a thin wire that, once in contact with its target, delivered an electric shock of up to 300,000 volts. The victim was immediately incapacitated by muscle spasms and intense pain. This crude weapon was used for crowd control or to subdue suspects of crimes.

When Ambassador for the New Humanity Mona Vaidyanathan first visited Steele, she asked what the queer black object was. Steele told her that it had been the most frequent means of communication between his father and himself. "When I was ten years old," he told her, "within a single month my father used that on me sixteen times."

"That's horrible," she said.

"Not for a person with a moral imagination," Steele replied.

In this new biography of Steele, Fiona 13, the Grand Lady of Reproductions, presents the crowning achievement of her long career recreating lives for the Cognosphere. Andrew Steele, when he died in 2100, had come to exemplify the twenty-first century, and his people, in a way that goes beyond the metaphorical. Drawing on every resource of the posthuman biographer, from heuristic modeling to reconstructive DNA sampling to forensic dreaming, Ms. 13 has produced this labor of, if not love, then obsession, and I for one am grateful for it.

Fiona presents her new work in a hybrid form. Comparatively little of this biography is subjectively rendered. Instead, harking back to a bygone era, Fiona breaks up the narrative with long passages of *text*—strings of printed code that must be read with the eyes. Of course this adds the burden of learning the code to anyone seeking to experience her recreation, but an accelerated prefrontal intervention is packaged with the biography. Fiona maintains that *text*, because it forces an artificial linearity on experience, stimulates portions of the left brain that seldom function in conventional experiential biographies. The result is that the person undergoing the life of Andrew Steele both lives through significant moments in Steele's subjectivity, and is drawn out of the stream of sensory and emotional reaction to contemplate the significance of that experience from the point of view of a wise commentator.

I trust I do not have to explain the charms of this form to those of you reading this review, but I recommend the experience to all cognizant entities who still maintain elements of curiosity in their affect repertoire.

CHILD

Appropriately for a man who was to so personify the twenty-first century, Dwight Andrew Steele was born on January 1, 2001. His mother, Rosamund Sanchez Steele, originally from Mexico, was a lab technician at the forestry school at North Carolina State University; his father, Herbert Matthew Steele, was a land developer and on the board of the Planter's Bank and Trust. Both of Steele's parents were devout Baptists and attended one of the "big box" churches that had sprung up in the late twentieth in response to growing millennialist beliefs in the United States and elsewhere.

The young Steele was "home schooled." This meant that Steele's mother devoted a portion of every day to teaching her son herself. The public school system was distrusted by large numbers of religious believers, who considered education by the state to be a form of indoctrination in moral error. Home schoolers operated from the premise that the less contact their children had with the larger world, the better.

Unfortunately, in the case of Andrew this did not prevent him from meeting other children. Andrew was a small, serious boy, sensitive, and an easy target for bullies. This led to his first murder. Fiona 13 realizes this event for us through extrapolative genetic mapping.

> *We are in the playground, on a bright May morning. We are running across the crowded asphalt toward a climbing structure of wood and metal, when suddenly we are falling! A nine-year-old boy named Jason Terry has tripped us and, when we regain our feet, he tries to pull our pants down. We feel the sting of our elbows where they scraped the pavement; feel surprise and dismay, fear, anger. As Terry leans forward to grab the waistband of our trousers, we suddenly bring our knee up into Terry's face. Terry falls back, sits down awkwardly. The other children gathered laugh. The sound of the laughter in our ears only enrages us more—are they laughing at us? The look of dismay turns to rage on Terry's face. He is going to beat us up, now; he is a deadly threat. We step forward, and before Terry can stand, kick him full in the face. Terry's head snaps back and strikes the asphalt, and he is still.*
>
> *The children gasp. A trickle of blood flows from beneath Terry's ear. From across the playground comes the monitor's voice: "Andrew? Andrew Steele?"*

I have never experienced a more vivid moment in biography. There it all is: the complete assumption by Steele that he is the victim. The fear and rage. The horror, quickly repressed. The later remorse, swamped by desperate justifications.

It was only through his father's political connections and acquiescence in private counseling (that the Steeles did not believe in, taking psychology as a particularly pernicious form of modern mumbo jumbo) that Andrew was kept out of the legal system. He withdrew into the family, his father's discipline and his mother's teaching.

More trouble was to follow. Keeping it secret from his family, Herbert Steele had invested heavily in real estate in the late oughts; he had leveraged properties he purchased to borrow money to invest in several hedge funds, hoping to put the family into a position of such fundamental wealth that they would be beyond the reach of economic vagaries.

When the Friends of the American League set off the Atlanta nuclear blast in 2012, pushing the first domino of the Global Economic Meltdown, Steele senior's financial house of cards collapsed. The US government, having spent itself into bankruptcy and dependence on Asian debt support through ill-advised imperial schemes and paranoid reactions to global terrorist threats, had no resources to deal with the collapse of private finance. Herbert Steele struggled to deal with the reversal, fell into a depression, and died when he crashed a borrowed private plane into a golf course in Southern Pines.

Andrew was twelve years old. His mother, finding part time work as a data entry clerk, made barely enough money to keep them alive. Andrew was forced into the public schools. He did surprisingly well there. Andrew always seemed mature for his years, deferential to his elders, responsible, trustworthy, and able to see others' viewpoint. He was slightly aloof from his classmates, and seemed more at home in the presence of adults.

Unknown to his overstressed mother, Andrew was living a secret life. On the Internet, under a half dozen false IP addresses, he maintained political websites. Through them he became one of the world's most influential "bloggers."

A blog was a personal web log, a site on the worldwide computer system where individuals, either anonymously or in their own names, commented on current affairs or their own lives. Some of these weblogs had become prominent, and their organizers and authors politically important.

Andrew had a fiction writer's gift for inventing consistent personalities, investing them with brilliant argument and sharp observation. On the *Political Theater* weblog, as Sacré True, he argued for the impeachment of President Harrison; on *Reason Season*, as Tom Pain, he demonstrated why Harrison's impeachment would prove disastrous. Fiona sees this phase of Steele's life as his education in manipulating others' sensibilities. His emotion-laden arguments were astonishingly successful at twisting his interlocutors into rhetorical knots. To unravel and respond to one of Steele's arguments rationally would take four times his space, and carry none of his propagandistic force. Steele's argument against the designated hitter rule even found its way into the platform of the resurgent Republican Party.

INTERROGATOR

"You don't know why I acted, but I know why. I acted because it is necessary for me to act, because that's what, whether you like it or not, you require me to do. And I don't mind doing it because it's what I have to do. It's what I was born to do. I've never been appreciated for it but that's okay too because, frankly, no one is ever appreciated for what they do.

"But before you presume to judge me realize that you are responsible. I am simply your instrument. I took on the burden of your desires when I didn't want to—I would just as gladly have let that cup pass me by—but I did it, and I have never complained. And I have never felt less than proud of what I have done. I did what was necessary, for the benefit of others. If it had been up to me I would never have touched a single human being, but I am not complaining.

"I do however ask you, humbly, if you have any scrap of decency left, if you have any integrity whatsoever, not to judge me. You do not have that right.

"Ask Carlo Sanchez, ask Alfonso Garadiana, ask Sayid Ramachandran, ask Billy Chen. Ask them what was the right thing to do. And then, when you've got the answer from their bleeding corpses, then, and only then, come to me."

—Andrew Steele, 2020
Statement before Board of Inquiry

Contemporary readers must remember the vast demographic and other circumstantial differences that make the early twenty-first century an alien land to us. When Steele was sixteen years old, the population of the world was an astonishing 6.8 billion, fully half of whom were under the age of twenty-five, the overwhelming majority of those young and striving individuals living in poverty, but with access, through the technologies that had spread widely over the previous twenty years, to unprecedented unregulated information. Few of them could be said to have been adequately acculturated. The history of the next forty years, including Steele's part in that history, was shaped by this fact.

In 2017 Steele was conscripted into the US Army pursuing the Oil War on two continents. Because he was fluent in Spanish, he served as an interrogator with the Seventy-First Infantry Division stationed in Venezuela. His history as an interrogator included the debriefing of the rightfully elected president of that nation in 2019. Fiona puts us there:

> *We are standing in the back of a small room with concrete walls, banks of fluorescent lights above, a HVAC vent and exposed ducts hanging from the ceiling. The room is cold. We have been standing for a long time and our back is stiff. We have seen many of these sessions, and all we can think about right now is getting out of here, getting a beer, and getting some sleep.*
>
> *In the center of the room Lieutenant Haslop and a civilian contractor are interrogating a small brown man with jet-black shoulder-length hair. Haslop is very tall and stoop shouldered, probably from a lifetime of*

ducking responsibility. The men call him "Slop" behind his back.

The prisoner's name is Alfonso Garadiana. His wrists are tied together behind him, and the same rope stretches down to his ankles, also tied together. The rope is too short, so that the only way he can stand is with his knees flexed painfully. But every time he sways, as if to fall, the contractor signals Haslop, who pokes him with an electric prod. Flecks of blood spot Garadiana's once brilliant white shirt. A cut over his eyebrow is crusted with dried blood, and the eye below it is half-closed.

The contractor, Mr. Gray, is neat and shaved and in control. "So," he says in Spanish, "where are the Jacaranda virus stores?"

Garadiana does not answer. It's unclear whether he has even understood.

Gray nods to Haslop again.

Haslop blinks his eyes, swallows. He slumps into a chair, rests his brow in one hand. "I can't do this anymore," he mutters, only apparently to himself. He wouldn't say it aloud if he didn't want us to hear it, even if he doesn't know that himself. We are sick to death of his weakness.

We step forward and take the prod from his hand. "Let me take care of this, sir." We swing the back of our hand against Garadiana's face, exactly the same motion we once used to hit a backhand in high school tennis. The man's head snaps back, and he falls to the floor. We move in with the prod.

Upon the failure of the Oil War and the defeat of the government that pursued it, a reaction took place, including war-crimes investigations that led to Steele's imprisonment from 2020 to 2025. Fiona gives us a glimpse of Steele's sensorium in his third year in maximum-security prison:

> We're hungry. Above us the air rattles from the ventilator. On the table before us in our jail cell is a notebook. We are writing our testament. It's a distillation of everything we know to be absolutely true about the human race and its future. There are things we know in our DNA that cannot be understood by strict rationality, though reason is a powerful tool and can help us to communicate these truths to those who do not, because of incapacity or lack of experience, grasp them instinctively.
>
> The blogs back when we were fourteen were just practice. Here, thanks to the isolation, we are able to go deep, to find the roots of human truth and put them down in words.
>
> We examine the last sentence we have written: "It is the hero's fate to be misunderstood."
>
> A guard comes by and raps the bars of our cell. "Still working on the great opus, Andy?"
>
> We ignore him, close the manuscript, move from the table, and begin to do push-ups in the narrow space beside the cot.
>
> The guard raps again on the bars. "How about an answer, killer?" His voice is testy.
>
> We concentrate on doing the push-ups correctly. Eleven. Twelve. Thirteen. Fourteen . . .

When we get out of here, all this work will make a difference.

This was indeed the case, Fiona shows us, but not in the way that Steele intended. As a work of philosophy his testament was rejected by all publishers. He struggled to make a living in the Long Emergency that was the result of the oil decline and the global warming-spawned environmental disasters that hit with full force in the 2020s. These changes were asymmetric, but though some regions felt them more than others, none were unaffected. The flipping of the Atlantic current turned 2022 into the first Year Without a Summer in Europe. Torrential rains in North Africa, the desertification of the North American Great Plains, mass wildlife migrations, drastic drops in grains production, die-offs of marine life, and decimated global fish stocks were among only the most obvious problems with which worldwide civilization struggled. And Andrew Steele was out of prison, without a connection in the world.

ARTIST

"The great artist is a rapist. It is his job to plant a seed, an idea or an emotion, in the viewer's mind. He uses every tool available to enforce his will. The audience doesn't know what it wants, but he knows what it wants, and needs, and he gives it to them.

"To the degree I am capable of it, I strive to be a great artist."

—Andrew Steele, 2037

"Man of Steele"
Interview on *VarietyNet*

At this moment of distress, Steele saw an opportunity, and turned his political testament into a best-selling novel, *What's Wrong with Heroes?* A film deal followed immediately. Steele insisted on being allowed to write the screenplay, and against its better judgment, the studio relented. Upon its release, *What's Wrong with Heroes?* became the highest grossing film in the history of cinema. In the character of Roark McMaster, Steele created a virile philosopher king who spoke to the desperate hopes of millions. With the money he made, Steele conquered the entertainment world. A series of blockbuster films, television series, and virtual adventures followed. This photo link shows him on the set of *The Betrayal*, his historical epic of the late twentieth century. The series, conflating the Vietnam War with two Iraq wars, presents the fiascos of the early twenty-first as the result of Machiavellian subversives and their bad-faith followers taking advantage of the innocence of the American populace, undermining what was once a strong and pure-minded nation.

Fiona gives us a key scene from the series:

INT. AMERICAN AIRLINES FLIGHT 11—DAY

Two of the hijackers, wearing green camo, are gathered around a large man seated in the otherwise empty first-class cabin of the 757. The big man, unshaven, wears a shabby Detroit Tigers baseball cap.

                    WALEED
                   (frantic)
              What shall we do now?

                    MOORE
         Keep the passengers back in coach. Is
         Mohammad on course? How long?

                  ABDULAZIZ
             (calling back from cockpit)
           Allah willing—three minutes.

[MOORE glances out the plane window.]
[MOORE's POV—through window, an aerial view of
Manhattan on a beautiful clear day]
[Close on MOORE. He smirks.]

                    MOORE
                  Time to go.

[MOORE hefts his bulk from the first-class seat, moves
toward the onboard baggage closet near the front of
the plane.]

                  ABDULAZIZ
              What are you doing?

[From out of a hanging suit bag, MOORE pulls a para-
chute, and straps it on.]

WALEED

Is this part of the plan?

[MOORE jerks up the lever on the plane's exterior door and yanks on it. It does not budge.]

MOORE

Don't just stand there, Waleed! Help me!

[WALEED moves to help MOORE, and reluctantly Abdulaziz joins them.]

ATTA

(from cockpit)

There it is! Allahu akbar!

[MOORE and the other two hijackers break the seal and the door flies open. A blast of wind sucks Abdulaziz and Waleed forward; they fall back onto the plane's deck. Moore braces himself against the edge of the door with his hands.

MOORE

In the name of the Democratic Party, the compassionate, the merciful—so long, boys!

[MOORE leaps out of the plane.]

The Betrayal was the highest-rated series ever to run on American television and cemented Steele's position as the most bankable mass-appeal Hollywood producer since Steven Spielberg. At the age of thirty-eight, Steele married the actress Esme Napoli, leading lady in three of his most popular films.

RELIGIOUS LEADER

The next section of Fiona's biography begins with this heartrending experience from Steele's middle years:

> *We are in a sumptuous hotel suite with a blonde woman who is not wearing much of anything. We are chasing her around the bed.*
>
> *"You can't catch me!"*
>
> *We snag her around the waist and pull her onto the bed. "I've already caught you. You belong to me." We hold up her ring finger, with its platinum band. "You see?"*
>
> *"I'm full of nanomachines," she says breathlessly. "If you catch me you'll catch them."*
>
> *The Scarlet Plague has broken out in Los Angeles, after raging for a month in Brazil. We have fled the city with Esme and are holed up in this remote hotel in Mexico.*
>
> *"When are we going to have these children?" we ask her. "We need children. Six at least."*
>
> *"You're going to have to work harder than this to deserve six children," Esme says. "The world is a mess. Do we want to bring children into it?"*

"The world has always been a mess. We need to bring children into it because it's a mess." We kiss her perfect cheek.

But a minute later, as we make love, we spot the growing rash along the inside of Esme's thigh.

The death of Steele's wife came near the beginning of the plague decade, followed by the Sudden War and the Collapse. Fiona cites the best estimates of historiographers that, between 2040 and 2062 the human population of the Earth went from 8.2 to somewhat less than 2 billion. The toll was slightly higher in the less developed nations; on the other hand, resistance to the plagues was higher among humans of the tropical regions. This situation in the middle years of the century transformed the Long Emergency of 2020 to 2040—a condition in which civilization, although stressed, might still be said to function, and with which Steele and his generation had coped—into the Die-Off, in which the only aspect of civilization that might be said to function, even in the least affected regions, was a desperate triage.

One of the results of the Long Emergency had been to spark widespread religious fervor. Social and political disruptions had left millions searching for certitudes. Longevity breakthroughs, new medicine, genetic engineering, cyborging, and AI pushed in one direction, while widespread climactic change, fights against deteriorating civil and environmental conditions, and economic disruptions pushed in another. The young warred against the old, the rich against the poor. Reactionary religious movements raged on four continents. Interpreting the chaos of the twenty-first century in terms of eschatology was a winning business. Terrorism in the attempt to bring on utopia or the end of the world was a common reality. Steele, despite his grief, rapidly grasped that art, even popular art, had no role in this world. So he turned, readily, to religion.

> "Human evolution is a process of moral evolution. The thing that makes us different from animals is our understanding of the ethical implications of every action that we perform: those that we must perform, those that we choose. Some actions are matters of contingency, and some are matters of free will.
>
> "Evolution means we will eventually come to fill the universe. To have our seed spread far and wide. That is what we are here for. To engender those children, to bear them, to raise them properly, to have them extend their—and our—thought, creativity, joy, understanding, to every particle of the visible universe."
>
> —Andrew Steele, 2052
> Sermon in the Cascades

Steele's Church of Humanity grew rapidly in the 2040s; while the population died and cities burned, its membership more than doubled every year, reaching twenty million by 2050. Steele's credo of the Hero transferred easily to religious terms; his brilliantly orchestrated ceremonies sparked ecstatic responses; he fed the poor and comforted the afflicted, and using every rhetorical device at his command, persuaded his followers that the current troubles were the birth of a new utopian age, that every loss had its compensation, that sacrifice was noble, that reward was coming, that from their loins would spring a new and better race, destined to conquer the stars. Love was the answer.

His creed crossed every ethnic, racial, sexual, gender preference, class, and age barrier. Everyone was human, and all equal.

The Church of Humanity was undeniably successful in helping millions of people, not just in the United States but across the bleeding globe, deal with the horrors of the Die-Off. It helped them to rally in the face of unimaginable psychological and material losses. But it was not the only foundation for the recovery. By the time some semblance of order was restored to world affairs in the 2060s, genetically modified humans, the superbrights, were attempting to figure a way out of the numerous dead ends of capitalism, antiquated belief systems, and a dysfunctional system of nation-states. This was a period of unexampled experimentation, and the blossoming of many technologies that had been only potentialities prior to the collapse, among them the uploading of human identities, neurological breakthroughs on the origins of altruism and violence, grafted information capacities, and free quantum energy.

Most of these developments presented challenges to religion. Steele came to see such changes as a threat to fundamental humanity. So began his monstrous political career.

POLITICIAN

"The greatest joy in life is putting yourself in the circumstance of another person. To see the world through his eyes, to feel the air on her skin, to breathe in deeply the spirit of their souls. To have their joy and trouble be equally real to you. To know that others are fully and completely human, just as you are. To get outside of your own subjectivity, and to see the world from a completely different and equally valid perspective, to come fully to understand them. When that point of understanding is reached, there is no other word for the feeling that you have than love. Just as much as you love yourself, as you love your children, you love this other.

"And at that point, you must exterminate them. That is the definition of difficult."

—Andrew Steele, 2071
What I Believe

Steele was swept into office as president of the reconstituted United States in the election of 2064, with his Humanity Party in complete control of the Congress. In his first hundred days, Steele signed a raft of legislation comprising his Humanity Initiative. Included were the Repopulation Act that forced all women of childbearing age to have no fewer than four children, a bold space colonization program, restrictions on genetic alterations and technological body modifications, the wiping clean of all uploaded personalities from private and public databases, the Turing Limit on AI, the Neurological Protection Act of 2065, and the establishment of a legal "standard human being."

In Steele's first term, "nonstandard" humans were allowed to maintain their civil rights, but were identified by injected markers, their movements and employment restricted by the newly established Humanity Agency. Through diplomatic efforts and the international outreach of the Church of Humanity, similar policies were adopted, with notable areas of resistance, throughout much of the world.

In Steele's second term, the HA was given police powers and the nonstandard gradually stripped of civil and property rights. By his third term, those who had not managed to escape the country lost all legal rights and were confined to posthuman reservations, popularly known as "Freak Towns." The establishment of the Protectorate over all of North and South America stiffened resistance elsewhere, and resulted in the uneasy Global Standoff. Eventually, inevitably, came the First and Second Human Wars.

Fiona includes a never-before-experienced moment from the twenty-third year of Steele's presidency.

> *We are in a command bunker, a large, splendidly appointed room, one whole wall of which is a breathtaking view of the Grand Tetons. We sit at a table with our closest advisors, listening to General Jinjur describe their latest defeat by the New Humans. There are tears in her eyes as she recounts the loss of the Fifth Army in the assault on Madrid.*
>
> *We do not speak. Our cat, Socrates, sits on our lap, and we scratch him behind his ears. He purrs.*
>
> *"How many dead?" Chief of Command Taggart asks.*
>
> *"Very few, sir," reports Jinjur. "But over ninety percent converted. It's their new amygdalic bomb. It's destroys our troops' will to fight. The soldiers just lay down their arms and go off looking for something to eat. You try organizing an autistic army."*

"At least they're good at math," says Secretary Bloom.

"How can these posthumans persist?" Dexter asks. "We've exterminated millions. How many of them are left?"

"We can't know, sir. The keep making more."

"But they don't even fight," says Taggart. "They must be on the point of extinction."

"It has never been about fighting, sir."

"It's this damned subversion," says Taggart. "We have traitors among us. They seed genetic changes among the people. They turn our own against us. How can we combat that?"

General Jinjur gathers herself. She is quite a striking woman, the flower of the humanity we have fought to preserve for so many years. "If I may be permitted to say so, we are fighting ourselves. We are trying to conquer our own human élan. Do you want to live longer? Anyone who wants to live longer will eventually become posthuman. Do you want to understand the universe? Anyone who wants to understand the universe will eventually become posthuman. Do you want peace of mind? Anyone who wants peace of mind will eventually become posthuman."

Something in her tone catches us, and we are finally moved to speak. "You are one of them, aren't you?"

"Yes," she says.

The contemporary citizen need not be troubled with, and Fiona does not provide, any detailed recounting of the war's progress, or how it ended in 2096 in the Peace that Passeth All

Understanding. The treatment of the remaining humans, the choices offered them, the removal of those few persisting to Mars, and their continued existence there under quarantine, are all material for another work.

Similarly, the circumstances surrounding Steele's death—the cross, the taser, the Shetland pony—so much a subject of debate, speculation and conspiracy theory, surely do not need rehearsing here. We know what happened to him. He destroyed himself.

AWAITING FURTHER INSTRUCTIONS

> "The highest impulse of which a human being is capable is to sacrifice himself in the service of the community of which he is a part, even when that community does not recognize him, and heaps opprobrium upon him for that sacrifice. In fact, such scorn is more often than not to be expected. The true savior of his fellows is not deterred by the prospect of rejection, though carrying the burden of his unappreciated gift is a trial that he can never, but for a few moments, escape. It is the hero's fate to be misunderstood."
>
> *What's Wrong with Heroes?* (unpublished version)

Fiona 13 ends her biography with a simple accounting of the number of beings, human and posthuman, who died as a result of Steele's life. She speculates that many of these same beings might not have lived had he not lived as well, and comes to no formal conclusion, utilitarian or otherwise, as to the moral consequences of the life of Dwight Andrew Steele.

Certainly few tears are shed for Andrew Steele, and few for the ultimate decline of the human race. I marvel at that remnant of humans who, using technologies that he abhorred, have incorporated into their minds a slice of Steele's personality in the attempt to make themselves into the image of the man they see as their savior. Indeed, I must confess to more than a passing interest in their poignant delusions, their comic, mystifying pastimes, their habitual conflicts, their simple loves and hates, their inability to control themselves, their sudden and tragic enthusiasms.

Bootlegged Steele personalities circulate in the Cognosphere, and it may be that those of you who, like me, on occasion edit their capacities in order to spend recreational time being human, will avail themselves of this no doubt unique and terrifying experience.

"I Planned to Be an Astronomer"
John Kessel Interviewed by Terry Bisson

Ever go back to Buffalo?

I haven't been back to Buffalo since my mother died in 2011, but I keep intending to do so. My brother, a flock of nieces. and my nephew live there, and I'd like to reacquaint myself with the place. It's always somewhere in my heart. The house my father started building when I was born, and that was in our family until I was in my sixties, still stands—owned by other people now.

I have a lot of memories of growing up a working-class child of Polish and Italian immigrants. It imprinted me with the ethnic mix of the first half of the twentieth century. Industrial capitalism and unions. The Catholic Church, which included 60 percent of the people of Buffalo in the 1950s, was ever present in my youth. The Great Depression, World War II, and the New Deal all happened before I was born but seemed to be ongoing realities in my family. One reason I've written stories set in the early twentieth century is that I felt like I lived in it.

Your corner of the South is almost like New England, in that everywhere you turn there is a university. Has that worked for you?

I like the Research Triangle and have lived in Raleigh now for more than half my life. It draws people from all over the US and the world. I enjoyed teaching at NC State University, a major research institution, for forty years. Its closeness to UNC–Chapel Hill and Duke, the vibrant cultural life, the good friends I have made make it a very good place to live.

I'll never be a southerner but I have learned a lot by living in the South. It's harder to ignore race as a factor in American life down here the way it was passed over so significantly where I grew up, and that has been good for me.

Plus, North Carolina is a beautiful state. The Piedmont, the Blue Ridge mountains, the Outer Banks, the beaches down east.

Did you always plan to be an academic?
No. I planned to be an astronomer. I never considered that in order to be one I would probably have to be a college professor. The professor side of that, the teaching and academic life, was not something I spent time thinking about.

When I later, as an undergraduate, double majored in physics and English, I still didn't think in terms of being a professor. Even when I went to grad school in English at the University of Kansas, I didn't expect I would last long enough to get a PhD. I wanted to be an SF writer and, figuring that I would have a tough time making a living solely from that, was looking for whatever kind of job might support me while I wrote.

For three years, taking a break from doctoral studies, I was a copyeditor and news editor for Commodity News Services and Unicom News, economic wire services jointly owned by Knight Ridder Newspapers and UPI. I was good at copyediting and enjoyed the work, though it was high-pressure. A wire service serving commodities investors, unlike a newspaper, is on a continual deadline. I learned a lot about how capitalism and markets work in the real world while I was there.

But gradually (it took me nine years from my BA to my doctorate) I thought maybe I could be an academic if I could get a job Like Jim Gunn's[‡]—one where I did not have to write scholarly literary criticism to justify my existence. When I finished the doctorate, I took a shot at applying to universities and was terribly lucky to get the job at NC State, where I started in 1982.

It turned out that I was well suited in some ways to being an academic, although in others I felt like a spy in the English department, someone who was not there for the same reason that others were. I was one of the last generation to be trained in the New Criticism in a literary history–based PhD program; I learned very little about the postmodern schools of criticism—structuralism, poststructuralism, deconstruction, Lacanian psychoanalytic criticism, semiotics, new Marxism, reader-response theory—those schools of heavily theoretical criticism that were to dominate English studies for most of my career. In grad school I wrote a lot of papers and did a lot of close reading for courses I took, but my interests were always in fiction writing. I would not have finished a PhD if I had not been able to persuade the KU English Department to allow me to write a creative writing dissertation.

And I discovered that I could be a good teacher. I've genuinely enjoyed teaching both literature and writing, sharing my enthusiasms with young people, working with writers hoping to get

---

[‡] James E. Gunn (1923–2020), American science fiction writer, editor, scholar, teacher, anthologist. Gunn taught writing and literature at the University of Kansas for fifty years and founded the Center for the Study of Science Fiction.

better. Learning how to teach writing improved my own writing. Even though I can't take any credit, I do feel great satisfaction when one of my former students publishes a book.

What did Kansas and Gunn give you? What was he like? Did you get to know any of the other old-timers?

Through my years of grad study at KU I learned a lot about classic literature; I read tons of things from *Beowulf* to Chaucer to the Renaissance poets and Elizabethan playwrights, the history of the novel in England and the US, twentieth-century British and American lit, contemporary fiction. I was ignorant and soaked this stuff up like a sponge. I liked most of it but learned from even those works I didn't like. From the scholar Elizabeth Schultz I got my love of Herman Melville. Studying lit gave me models to aspire to.

Jim Gunn was a living example of the history of SF from the 1940s on, the last of the Mohicans in that way. He wrote science fiction and about science fiction. He knew everybody of the generation of writers who came of age in the 1950s and through him I met many of them: Brian Aldiss, Fred Pohl, Theodore Sturgeon, Gordon Dickson, John Brunner, Ben Bova, Samuel Delany, Harlan Ellison—all of them visited KU at one point or another while I was there. I was Gunn's grad assistant and therefore had to pick visiting writers up at the Kansas City airport and drive them back to Lawrence. I could ask them questions, talk about SF and writing it—though I was shy and did not want to annoy them. Some of them guest taught workshops and critiqued my stories.

Jim directed my master's thesis in fiction writing and was on my PhD committee when I wrote a creative writing dissertation.

(I was one of three students who managed to get creative writing dissertations past the grad school in the early 1980s before they objected to such silliness and closed down the option.)

Jim read everything I wrote and commented on it. He was a tough reader. I was writing what was called New Wave SF at that time—my heroes were Ursula Le Guin, Thomas Disch, Gene Wolfe, Kate Wilhelm—and Jim was an old-school John W. Campbell/Horace Gold writer. He forced me to think about what I was doing, why I was doing it, how a story was constructed, and how it might be made better. "Stories aren't written," he said, "they're rewritten." I did not take to this immediately, though I came eventually to find revision the most rewarding part of the process.

He invited me into his home and was kind to me. Jim had a certain Midwestern reserve that was hard to get past. He believed in science fiction as a way to shape the future; for him SF was about ideas, and should have a positive effect on the world. I was more of a cynic and a skeptic. I always had a Kurt Vonnegut satirical side. But we both believed in reason and thought that SF was literature, not just disposable entertainment, and should be written to high standards. He was a good role model. I've tried to be as patient with my students as he was with me.

I visited eastern Kansas several times when I was obsessed with and writing about John Brown. Was Brown actually much of a presence there?

I don't remember Brown being a presence in the life of the people I lived among in Kansas and Missouri, even though the things he cared about shaped so much of the place and are still live issues.

But that John Steuart Curry mural in the Kansas State Capitol is astonishing.

John Brown lives! Smash white supremacy!

How did Sycamore Hill come about?

In 1980 and '81 I was living in Kansas City and Ed Bryant invited me to the Milford workshops that he ran in Colorado. Those were formative experiences for me. I had published only a handful of stories at that point. I'd admired Ed's work for years and at the workshop I met Connie Willis, Cynthia Felice, George R.R. Martin, Steve and Melanie Tem, and Dan Simmons, among others. For the first time I felt like I might belong to a community of writers.

When I moved to Raleigh I became friends with Mark Van Name and Gregory Frost, who were also early in their careers. Mark moved into a new house in the mid-1980s and Greg casually observed that it was big enough to hold a workshop in, so in January 1985 Mark and I organized a five-day workshop along the Milford model. All the writers who came were men, most of them from North Carolina. It seemed to work well, so the next year we moved it to a house we rented on the campus of the Governor Morehead School in Raleigh, expanded it to a full week, and invited writers from all over the country, including Jim Kelly, Bruce Sterling, Orson Scott Card, Karen Joy Fowler, Susan Palwick, Rebecca Ore, and others. The thing turned into a yearly workshop.

This was in the midst of the regrettable cyberpunk-humanist business. I was interested in trying to get some of the most ambitious and outspoken writers of my generation together in the same room to see whether we might have a productive exchange of ideas and support each other in our different ways of writing good SF. Most of the participants took to this idea, but some were not able to communicate across the natural divides that exist between writers. That was a learning experience.

Mark and I ran SycHill until the mid-1990s in Raleigh, then it went on hiatus for a few years, to be resurrected later at Bryn Mawr College in Philadelphia, run by Richard Butner and me with the help of Greg Frost, who had moved there. Later we moved to the Wildacres Retreat Center in the Blue Ridge Mountains of NC, where it still continues. In 2006 I handed it off to Richard, who has run it very successfully ever since. He's changed a number of elements, in my mind much for the better. I just got home yesterday from the 2023 Sycamore Hill.

Were you ever published in the Whole Earth Catalog? *I was.*
Nope. I used to read it back in my counterculture days.

If you could live in any city for a year (comfortably), which would it be?
There are a lot of cities I'd love to try that with. London, Berlin, Prague, Rome, Paris. San Francisco. Seattle.

One sentence or so on each, please: Guy Davenport, Kelly Reichardt, J.D. Crowe.
To my embarrassment, I have never read anything by Guy Davenport.

To my embarrassment, I have never seen a film by Kelly Reichardt.

To my embarrassment, I have never seen a performance by J.D. Crowe.

What poets do you read for improvement?
Among contemporaries I love the work of my colleagues Dorianne Laux and Joe Millar. Gerald Barrax, a wonderful poet, was my colleague at NC State for many years. I like Stephen Dunn. I like Hafez. Rilke. I love all sorts of classic poetry: Donne, Blake, Dickinson, Frost, Eliot, Williams. I come back to Yeats all the time.

I've tried writing a few poems myself but can't say I've gone deeply into that place. Something always pulls me toward narrative. But nothing is more powerful than the distilled shock you get from poetry.

Funny how serious New Englanders (Small Beer Press) seem to have an affinity with your little knot of southern writers (Rowe, Butner, et al.). Explain.
Throw in Andy Duncan (*An Agent of Utopia*). Kelly Link has North Carolina connections, so maybe that has something to do with it, but I rather doubt that.

Christopher (*Telling the Map*) and Richard (*The Adventurists*) and I (*The Baum Plan for Financial Independence*) are excellent writers of short fiction that fits into the offbeat sensibilities of Small Beer Press. Christopher's fiction has deep roots in the South, as does Andy's. I don't see as much of the South in Richard's. And as I said above, even though I've lived in the South for a long time and have set a few stories here, I don't consider myself a southern writer.

I suppose that accidents of encounters with each other may have had something to do with it. If Small Beer likes the South, they like the weird South.

I found Pride and Prometheus *impressive and serious in spite of the silly title. Was the excellence of the Austen fabric scholarship or affection?*

On some days I think *Pride and Prometheus* is my best novel, or at least has my best protagonist, Mary Bennet. I am a big fan of Austen's fiction, but since I am an Americanist, I have never taught any of her work—though I've taught *Frankenstein*, the other inspiration for my novel, many times.

I'm not an Austen scholar, but I love her novels. She so smart and funny, but also wickedly cynical. I read her books for the dark observations on British society that flow through them, but also for fun. I would say the book was powered by affection more than scholarship.

I was also drawn to fusing Shelley with Austen because they represent two major streams of literature in English. *Frankenstein* is a foundational text for science fiction, as Austen is for the modern novel of manners. Since I have spent much of my career trying to cross the sensibilities of these two forms of fiction, it was irresistible to me to try to draw these stories together. They don't naturally fit together; my novel starts in Austenland and gradually moves into the gothic as Mary Bennet falls out of the polite, privileged society, where she was born, into the madness and extremity of Shelley's novel.

Some Austen fans have complained that no woman of 1815 could have undergone the degradations I put my Mary Bennet through, but of course there were countless women in England at that time who suffered much worse. What those readers mean is that the people of the lower classes who lived those hard lives are invisible in Austen's novels. Such readers are complaining that my novel slips from one genre to another, and they don't want that. I don't give a happily-ever-after ending.

One of the unfortunate facts about the reception of *Pride and Prometheus* is that many readers, hearing the premise (a novel that crosses characters from *Pride and Prejudice* with the story of *Frankenstein*) think it must be a joke along the lines of the execrable *Pride and Prejudice and Zombies*. It is, as you say, a serious novel (with some attempts at Austenian humor, it's true).

One of the things I wanted to do in it was to present Mary Bennet as something more than the figure of fun that she is in Austen's novel. Flaubert said, "Madame Bovary, c'est moi." I say, "I am Mary Bennet."

One of SF's famous friendships is you and Jim Kelly. What's the story there?
I just spent a week rooming with him at Sycamore Hill. Somebody at the workshop asked if we had ever had a falling out. We scratched our heads and could not come up with anything. We may have had a disagreement here and there but nothing that has touched our friendship.

We met at the World SF Convention in Boston in 1980 when I noticed his name tag while I waited for an elevator and realized he was the author of a story I'd recently read and admired, "Death Therapy." He told me I was the first person who had ever recognized him as a writer. I liked his fiction from the start; he seemed to me to be smart and funny and full of invention, and he was writing things that I would have been proud to write myself.

We had similarities of background and temperament. Both raised Catholic but lapsed, both New Wave fans, both from New York State, graduated from college with English degrees the same year. I liked him as a person and as a writer. We exchanged manuscripts and offered comments to each other, talked writing and careers. We collaborated on some stories and then a novel. By the mid-1980s we had attended so many conventions together we got nicknamed the glimmer twins of humanist SF. Our careers have gone forward more or less in parallel, though we do not write as much alike as we did in 1985.

Even though we've never lived within seven hundred miles of each other, he is my dearest friend.

Your work has made it into film several times. How has that worked for you?

Only once: my story "A Clean Escape" was made into the first episode of the very short-lived anthology series *Masters of Science Fiction*. The script was by producer Sam Egan; it was directed by Mark Rydell and starred Judy Davis and Sam Waterston. Though it is expanded from my story, it does contain scenes that are right out of the story. I got to go up to Vancouver and see the episode filmed. It was cool to see my dialogue spoken by those actors.

I've had an option taken for a series titled *Clean* based on a couple of my stories. But no production yet.

You may have thought I had something else adapted because I had the pleasure of acting in a film: *The Delicate Art of the Rifle*, directed by Dante Harper, written by a former student of mine,

Stephen Grant, and shot on the NCSU campus in 1994. It's inspired by the tower sniper, Charles Whitman, who killed fourteen people at the University of Texas in the mid-1960s. I play Dr. Max Boaz, a rather weird college professor.[§]

Did you teach writing or literature other than SF & fantasy?
Yes. I was hired to teach both American literature and creative writing, and for my first twenty years at NC State most of my teaching was in literature. Besides separate courses on SF and fantasy, I regularly taught the two-semester American literature survey and courses on major American writers. My students were mostly non-English majors taking them to fulfill a humanities requirement. I relished the opportunity to be the last English teacher most of them would ever have. I considered it my job to leave them with the idea that reading old books and poems might actually have some relevance to their own lives—and that it could be considered a peculiar sort of *fun.*

I suspect that most of your students at NC State were actual (born-and-raised) southerners. What did you learn from them?
That the South is a more complicated place than I had imagined it was in my ignorance before I moved here. Plus, it's possible to like both Kansas City and North Carolina barbecue.

What are you reading these days?

---

§   Dante Harper, director, clip from *The Delicate Art of the Rifle*, YouTube video, February 27, 2021, 10:44, https://www.youtube.com/watch?v=qucMpuFrFlA.

Except for research reading for fiction—and I do a lot of that—since I've retired from teaching, I read haphazardly. Some old books, some new ones, some in genre and many without. I keep a list of books I've read. Among those from recent months are *Creatures of Will and Temper* by Molly Tanzer, *Cora Crane: A Biography of Mrs. Stephen Crane* by Lillian Gilkes, *The Strange* by Nathan Ballingrud, *Crooked, but Never Common* by Stewart Klawans, and *A Visit from the Goon Squad* by Jennifer Egan.

What car do you drive? How come? I ask this of everyone.
I drive a 2018 Audi E-tron Sportback, a plug-in hybrid that I bought used about a year ago. It's the most fun-to-drive car I have ever owned. Before this I'd been driving underpowered Hondas since the 1970s.

I like it because it's environmentally friendly, relatively small, accelerates quickly when I need it to, and looks snazzy.

Ever write for comics?
When I started out in the late 1970s I scripted a comic strip, *Crosswhen*, a collaboration with my Kansas City friend Terry Lee, that appeared in *Galileo* from 1978 until the magazine's demise several years later. I can't speak for the quality of my scripts, but it was fun to write.

You have pretty explicit and progressive politics. Is the Right right about anything?
That's a good question. The political right in the US today is appalling and my instincts are to say no, but when I look at it more objectively I can say that some of the things that the classic right

professes to believe in, such as individual responsibility, should be incorporated into any mature political understanding. That doesn't contradict, in my mind, the necessity for government to curb capitalism, protect the environment, insure social, racial, and economic justice, preserve democratic elections and institutions, and plan for a future that goes beyond the next quarterly earnings report. In the capitalist world we live in government is the only force large enough to counter the immense power of corporations and the wealthy.

Are you prepared for the Singularity?
The singularity is a fantasy, or at best a metaphor. So I guess if it happens, I will be unprepared.

A Brief History of the War with Venus

CHARACTERS

THE PRESIDENT of the Solar Federation
JAMISON (pronounced JAMM-iss-son), his aide, an android
THE AMBASSADOR from Venus

SETTING

The office of the President of the Solar Federation

TIME

A couple of centuries from now

At rise: The PRESIDENT, a man who might have been handsome thirty years earlier, sits behind his massive desk. On the desk are a pad, a pen, a green communicator/phone, a button. Behind him, a large view port looks out on a vivid starscape, with a gibbous moon shining like a beacon.

On one side of the stage is the door to the office, on the other an airlock door. The purple Flag of the Solar System hangs in the corner.

The PRESIDENT, leaning back with his feet on the desk, wearing a space helmet. He periodically eyes the communicator, nervously.

[PRESIDENT humming a song. Begins to sing, to the tune of Gilbert & Sullivan's "A Modern Major General"]

PRESIDENT

I am the modern model of a very stable gee-nee-us,

I rule with smarts and scheming and the biggest ever pee-nee-us

In thinking up distractions that are anything but practical

There is no greater leader in the realms of the galactical—

[A knock on the door]

PRESIDENT

Go away!

[Another, more persistent knock]

PRESIDENT

This is my Presidentiary Time! I'm working. I'm working very hard. Leave me alone!

JAMISON

Mr. President, it's me, Jamison!

[PRESIDENT takes off space helmet, holds it.]

PRESIDENT
(grumpily)

Oh, all right, come in.

[Enter JAMISON]

JAMISON
(urgently)

Mr. President—

PRESIDENT
(idly examining the helmet)
Jamison, did I ever tell you the history of this space helmet?

JAMISON

Mr. President, I have someone here to see you. It's urgent—

PRESIDENT

I was a young man, supervising the construction of a bunch of multiuse habitats on Mercury. It gets hot on Mercury.

JAMISON

So I understand. But I think you should meet with—

PRESIDENT
(still fondling helmet)
There was a containment breach. Loss of oxygen. You can bet I hightailed it out of there *toot sweet*! I gave the survivors vouchers for zero-G golf at our L-5 resort. In return they gave me this helmet.

I'm just sentimental, I guess, hanging on to it. Though you never know when a space helmet is going to come in handy—that's why I keep it right here by the executive airlock.

Now what is it that's so important that you have to interrupt my vital Presidentiary Time?

JAMISON

Sir, I'm afraid we have a serious problem. Reports are that Venus has left its orbit.

[PRESIDENT puts helmet down on desk, suddenly engaged.]

PRESIDENT

You're kidding.

JAMISON

I'm an android, sir. I never kid.

PRESIDENT

What happened?

JAMISON

It's hard to say as yet. I think it might trace back to your building that resort at the Venusian pole. The one that required changing the climate? All those orbiting sun shields to lower the temperature?

PRESIDENT

We call that terraforming, Jamison. I know all about terraforming. Nobody knows more about terraforming than I do.

JAMISON

Well, changing the climate produced a lot of Venusian refugees, so you started quarantining Venusian immigrants on the Moon?

PRESIDENT

That was a stupendous idea. I had that idea. Everybody loves that idea.

JAMISON

Yes, Mr. President, but—

PRESIDENT

Even the Venusians. The *good* Venusians.

JAMISON

Yes, sir.

PRESIDENT

The *good* Venusians loved that idea. They love me.

JAMISON

There are schools of thought on that, Mr. President—

PRESIDENT

Some of my best friends are from other planets.

JAMISON

I don't doubt it, sir.

PRESIDENT

After my second wife dissolved, I even dated a Venusian for a while.

JAMISON

Concentrate, Mr. President.

PRESIDENT

I am concentrating! I'm the best concentrator!

JAMISON

You'll recall then that the underground lunar colonies couldn't house all the refugees, so you threw up those temporary domes on the surface. You put your son in charge of the project. But the domes' radiation shielding was substandard.

PRESIDENT

I didn't put Junior in charge to waste taxpayer money on refugees. He concentrates almost as well as I do.

JAMISON

When that solar storm happened last year—

PRESIDENT

The Solar Emergency Management Agency was all over that. I went out of my way to help those greenies. It was a triumph!

JAMISON

Yes, sir. No one who saw it would argue that your performance was not remarkable. The video of you using that T-shirt cannon to fire rolled up lead radiation umbrellas to crowds of suffering refugees was heart rending.

PRESIDENT

If we had built the shield around the moon that I proposed during my campaign, then none of the Venusians could have even gotten there. None of this would have happened.

JAMISON

It wasn't practical, Mr. President. The amount of glassite it would take to enclose the moon in a sphere is astronomical.

PRESIDENT

Of course it's astronomical! This is outer space!

It seems to me lately you only give me reasons why I can't do what I want, Jamison. Is that your idea of being Aide to the President of the Solar Federation? Use your imagination!

JAMISON

(as much to himself as to the PRESIDENT)

Having an imagination sometimes makes this job harder.

PRESIDENT

I'm surrounded by traitors and incompetents! Here we are, orbiting high above the Earth in Solar City. We're standing in the Solar Palace. Look—there's the solar flag! This is a solar pen!

If we built the shield we could pump in air and give the Moon an atmosphere! But the traitorous Parliament refuses to pony up the money.

JAMISON

Senator Zipp doesn't trust you, sir. She claims you're under the tentacle of the Quarm of Saturn.

PRESIDENT

I don't even know the Quarm of Saturn. I've never met him.

JAMISON

"Them," sir—the Quarm is a group organism.

PRESIDENT

"He," "she," "them"—it's too confusing. If they care what we call them, they should have it tattooed on their forehead. Regardless, I've never met the thing.

JAMISON

Mr. President, actually, you met with the Quarm at the Martian Summit last year.

PRESIDENT

That was the Quarm? I thought it was an art installation.

JAMISON

Senator Zipp says that during that meeting the Quarm infected you and has gradually colonized your mind. She says they manipulate you like a puppet.

PRESIDENT

That's absurd, Jamison. [*Flaps his arms*] Do you see any strings—

[Communicator rings. PRESIDENT dashes to desk, picks it up.]

Hello? . . . Oh, hello—

[Covers his mouth and the communicator with his hand, cagily, turning away from JAMISON, lowering his voice]

I can't talk . . . just a minute.

[Takes pad and pen and begins to write notes]

Okay, then . . .

[Switches to much louder "public" voice]

Thanks, dear! I'll pick up that sushi after work. No problem!

[Hangs up, turns to JAMISON, flaps arms again]

So . . . not a puppet! Not a puppet! No strings!

JAMISON

No, sir. But the newsfeeds say that this would explain why you are so hard on the Venusians, Venus being the historic enemy of Saturn.

PRESIDENT

History is bunk!

This is nothing to worry about, Jamison. Most of the voters can't find Saturn on a star map.

(looking out the viewport)

Which one is Saturn again?

JAMISON

The one with the rings, sir. The Internal Affairs Committee of the Parliament is calling for you to submit to a complete body scan.

PRESIDENT

(sarcastically)

Oh, right. I'm sure they'd like to get up-close and personal with my body. Who wouldn't? That's the path to world domination! But it's not gonna happen.

Let's get back to this Venus thing.

JAMISON

Right, sir. So the number of casualties among the refugees is rising.

PRESIDENT

They should have stayed on their own planet.

JAMISON

Back on Venus they are not happy about it. Their premier is hopping mad.

PRESIDENT

I saw that on the Tri-Vid this morning. That gal can really hop! Must be the lower gravity.

JAMISON

Venus's gravity is the same as Earth's, Mr. President.

PRESIDENT

Oh.

(beat)

She must be really mad, then.

JAMISON

Yes, Mr. President. She's really mad.

PRESIDENT

Do we have any people there?

JAMISON

On Venus? . . . Not anymore.

PRESIDENT

Poor bastards.

JAMISON

The last we heard from our agents is that the Premier
mobilized the Venusian Army. And now the planet has
left its orbit. That's why I summoned their ambassador.
I think you should speak with her.

[JAMISON moves to office door, pauses there leaning out.
Meanwhile the PRESIDENT knots his hands behind his back and
paces back and forth. He is not paying attention to what JAMISON
is doing. After a moment, turning to the door, he waves his hand
dismissively.]

PRESIDENT

Don't worry about Venus, Jamison. Venus is a shithole
planet. Do they even have a space force?

[As he says this, JAMISON enters with the AMBASSADOR.]

AMBASSADOR

We don't need a space force.

JAMISON

Mr. President, the Ambassador of Venus.
[PRESIDENT recoils]

PRESIDENT

(to JAMISON)

What is she doing here?

AMBASSADOR
I'm here to negotiate the terms of your surrender.

PRESIDENT
Surrender? Pathetic! Maybe if you're extra nice we'll help you move your planet back into its orbit.

AMBASSADOR
We'll move it back ourselves—once we've conquered the Solar Federation.

PRESIDENT
Think again, missy. The Solar Federation has the largest space force that has ever existed. You can't imagine how big it is. It's very big. Huge.

AMBASSADOR
Not as big as a planet. We've weaponized our home world and turned it into a mobile battle station. As we speak, Venus hurtles toward us, armed and fortified as only a planet can be!

PRESIDENT
A whole planet as a weapon?
> (leans toward JAMISON)
Why don't we have one of those?

JAMISON
> (shakes head, sighing)
I hate this job.

PRESIDENT

(to AMBASSADOR)

Maybe we can strike a deal. We've got a lot of your people on the Moon. Suppose we cede the Moon to you? It's a pretty piece of real estate.

AMBASSADOR

No atmosphere.

PRESIDENT

It's a fixer-upper! Build a sphere around it and you can pump in an atmosphere.

AMBASSADOR

Sorry. It's unconditional surrender or complete annihilation.

PRESIDENT

Mars! How about Mars? It comes with *two* moons! They're small, but crunchy.

AMBASSADOR

The way a negotiation works is you have to offer us something we want. We don't want the Moon, or Mars.

PRESIDENT

Don't tell me how to negotiate! Ask the Quarm of Saturn about how tough a negotiator I am.

[As he speaks the PRESIDENT sidles over to his desk, picks up his space helmet.]

Meanwhile, I think I'll take a little spacewalk—as soon
as I blow open the airlock!

[PRESIDENT puts on the helmet, presses a button on his desk. A
sound of the airlock door being blown open and the rush of escap-
ing air.]

Suck vacuum, losers!

[PRESIDENT hops out the airlock door. AMBASSADOR backs out of
the office as the air escapes. JAMISON, backing up along with her,
cups hands to his mouth, calls after the PRESIDENT.]

JAMISON
Mr. President, it's a phony helmet! They gave you a
phony helmet!

[JAMISON watches as PRESIDENT recedes into the blackness of
space.]

(to himself)
A complete phony.

Bibliography

Novels

Pride and Prometheus. Saga Press, 2018.

The Moon and the Other. Saga Press, 2017.

Corrupting Dr. Nice. Tor Books, 1997.

Good News from Outer Space. Tor Books, 1989.

Another Orphan (novella). Tor Books, 1989.

Freedom Beach (with James Patrick Kelly). Bluejay Books, 1985

Collections

The Dark Ride. Subterranean Press, 2022.

The Baum Plan for Financial Independence and Other Stories.
   Small Beer Press, 2008.

The Pure Product. Tor Books, 1997.

Meeting in Infinity. Arkham House, 1992.

Anthologies

edited with James Patrick Kelly:

Digital Rapture: The Singularity Anthology. Tachyon Publications,
   2011.

Kafkaesque: Stores After Franz Kafka. Tachyon Publications,
   2011.

Nebula Award Showcase. Pyr Books, 2011.

The Secret History of Science Fiction. Tachyon Publications, 2009.
Rewired: The Post-Cyberpunk Anthology. Tachyon Publications,
2007.
Feeling Very Strange: The Slipstream Anthology. Tachyon
Publications, 2006.

edited with Mark L. Van Name and Richard Butner:
Intersections: The Sycamore Hill Anthology. Tor Books, 1996

About the Author

JOHN KESSEL HOLDS AN undergraduate degree in physics and English and a PhD in American literature. For many years he taught literature and creative writing at North Carolina State University in Raleigh, where he helped found the MFA program in creative writing. His fiction has twice received the Nebula Award, plus the Otherwise Award (formerly the James Tiptree Jr. Award), the Shirley Jackson Award, the Theodore Sturgeon Award, the Locus Award, and the Ignotus Award.

He lives in Raleigh with his wife, the author Therese Anne Fowler.

FRIENDS OF

PM

These are indisputably momentous times—the financial system is melting down globally and the Empire is stumbling. Now more than ever there is a vital need for radical ideas.

In the years since its founding—and on a mere shoestring—PM Press has risen to the formidable challenge of publishing and distributing knowledge and entertainment for the struggles ahead. With hundreds of releases to date, we have published an impressive and stimulating array of literature, art, music, politics, and culture. Using every available medium, we've succeeded in connecting those hungry for ideas and information to those putting them into practice.

Friends of PM allows you to directly help impact, amplify, and revitalize the discourse and actions of radical writers, filmmakers, and artists. It provides us with a stable foundation from which we can build upon our early successes and provides a much-needed subsidy for the materials that can't necessarily pay their own way. You can help make that happen—and receive every new title automatically delivered to your door once a month—by joining as a Friend of PM Press. And, we'll throw in a free T-shirt when you sign up.

Here are your options:
- $30 a month: Get all books and pamphlets plus 50% discount on all webstore purchases
- $40 a month: Get all PM Press releases (including CDs and DVDs) plus 50% discount on all webstore purchases
- $100 a month: Superstar—Everything plus PM merchandise, free downloads, and 50% discount on all webstore purchases

For those who can't afford $30 or more a month, we have Sustainer Rates at $15, $10, and $5. Sustainers get a free PM Press T-shirt and a 50% discount on all purchases from our website.

Your Visa or Mastercard will be billed once a month, until you tell us to stop. Or until our efforts succeed in bringing the revolution around. Or the financial meltdown of Capital makes plastic redundant. Whichever comes first.

PM Press is an independent, radical publisher of critically necessary books for our tumultuous times. Our aim is to deliver bold political ideas and vital stories to all walks of life and arm the dreamers to demand the impossible. Founded in 2007 by a small group of people with decades of publishing, media, and organizing experience, we have sold millions of copies of our books, most often one at a time, face to face. We're old enough to know what we're doing and young enough to know what's at stake. Join us to create a better world.

PM Press
PO Box 23912
Oakland, CA 94623
info@pmpress.org

PM Press in Europe
europe@pmpress.org
www.pmpress.org.uk

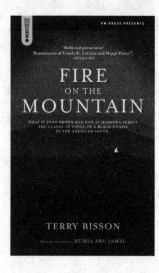

Fire on the Mountain

Terry Bisson
Introduction by Mumia Abu-Jamal
ISBN: 978-1-60486-087-0
208 pages • 5 x 8 • $18.95

It's 1959 in socialist Virginia. The Deep South is an independent Black nation called Nova Africa. The second Mars expedition is about to touch down on the red planet. And a pregnant scientist is climbing the Blue Ridge in search of her great-great grandfather, a teenage slave who fought with John Brown and Harriet Tubman's guerrilla army.

Long unavailable in the U.S., published in France as *Nova Africa*, *Fire on the Mountain* is the story of what might have happened if John Brown's raid on Harper's Ferry had succeeded—and the Civil War had been started not by the slave owners but the abolitionists.

> *"History revisioned, turned inside out . . . Bisson's wild and wonderful imagination has taken some strange turns to arrive at such a destination."*
> —Madison Smartt Bell, Anisfield-Wolf Award winner and author of *Devil's Dream*